THE
VALIANT
PAPERS

Other books by Calvin Miller

The Singer
The Song
The Finale

Burning Bushes and Moon Walks

Once Upon a Tree

The Philippian Fragment

Guardians of the Singreale

THE
VALIANT
PAPERS

Calvin Miller

Illustrations by Joe DeVelasco

ZONDERVAN
PUBLISHING HOUSE
OF THE ZONDERVAN CORPORATION
GRAND RAPIDS, MICHIGAN 49506

Second printing May 1982

Edited by James E. Ruark
Designed by Martha Bentley
Illustrations by Joe DeVelasco

Library of Congress Cataloging in Publication Data
Miller, Calvin.
    The valiant papers.

    I. Title.
PS3563.I376V3   813'.54   81-19724
ISBN 0-310-29291-3   AACR2

Printed in the United States of America

The Terminal Connection

One Friday night in April, I was traveling through Cleveland, Ohio. I was to change buses after a short layover and continue to Buffalo, New York. As we pulled into the terminal, I noticed a chartered bus filled with men and women who appeared to be somewhat older than college age. Through the large windows of the bus I could see they were sitting in a random fashion, not in the customary heterosexual arrangement of young marrieds. I assumed, therefore, that they were singles departing on some lark. I could not immediately think of the nature of their outing since it was too late for the ski season and too early for summer vacations.

One couple near the back window of the bus was strumming guitars and singing. As a pastor I have seen enough of guitars and young folk, and I suddenly realized it was a religious retreat in its formative stages.

Our buses passed slowly. The one on which I rode pulled into the gate that the charter had vacated. This turned out to be the most timely of departures and arrivals. I was shortly to make an amazing discovery.

I found myself sitting in the terminal with my briefcase under my seat. I leaned back against the sweater that I had removed. I was uncomfortably warm and feeling a touch of nausea which I attributed to the irregular motion of the bus in the heavy city traffic.

While waiting for the bus to Buffalo, I sat absent-mindedly running my hand over the empty seat next to the one I occupied. In this distracted activity my fingers fell upon a sticky surface. I thought it to be cola accidentally spilled by a clumsy child probably as impatient as I to board a bus.

I instinctively recoiled. Something from the seat clung to my finger tips. The stickiness was not a beverage slick as I had thought, but a piece of semi-adhesive cellophane the size of typing paper, except much thinner. When I held the transparency to the light, I could see that it was not entirely clear. It contained some characters nearly impossible to read. The tiny "glyphs" appeared to be a faded form of handwriting. I squinted in a vain attempt to make the queer etchings yield words, or even a single recognizable letter. They would not.

As I placed my hand upon the empty seat again, the sticky sensation recurred. Once more I drew back, and just as surely had lifted a second piece of this clear film bearing the same faint, unintelligible characters. I placed this second transparency behind the first and reached again to the empty seat. Another sheet adhered. Some thirty times I repeated the procedure until I had lifted and stacked everything that the seat contained. I arranged the sheets in exactly the order that I had retrieved them. When my hand finally fell on naked wood, I felt somehow cheated that the strange adventure was over.

My next activity must have appeared strange to others in the terminal. I rose and checked my own seat to be sure there were no sheets there. I moved along the row of empty chairs until I came to one occupied by a rather portly gentleman. He peered at me over the top of his newspaper in a way that unnerved me and halted my search.

I did not fold the sheets, but put them directly into my attaché case, planning to examine them later. As I placed them in the case, I took two aspirin from it and swallowed them, hoping to alleviate a headache that had grown to a dull throb during my stay in the terminal.

My bus was called at last. I grabbed my sweater and attaché case and walked to the gate. I boarded the bus still feeling nausea. My condition worsened as I began to feel alternately chills and fever. The long ride to Buffalo became one of the most arduous trips of my life.

Several times on the bus I fell asleep in a deep slumber that resembled a coma. In brief moments of consciousness I feared that I might be experiencing some sort of seizures. In spasms of unconsciousness it seemed I heard the wing-beats of some very large bird. In conscious moments I attributed these strange flutterings to the delirium of fever.

I prayed to be free of the sickness. But neither aspirin nor prayer offered deliverance. Several times I thought of asking the driver to stop and arrange my transportation to some hospital. But usually, by breathing deeply, I would feel some relief. In these better moments I felt embarrassed that I had thought myself to be sick at all.

Finally I arrived in Buffalo, took a cab to my hotel, and checked in. Weary, I started immediately to bed. However, my mind turned again to the sheets in my briefcase. My curiosity was greater than my weariness, so I unsnapped the latches.

The sticky sheets were still there. While they had not grown thicker, they were becoming more opaque. I was delighted to see that the characters which had been too dim to read grew more distinct as the papers lost their transparency. Most of all I was relieved to see that they were written in English. I could actually make out words and sentences. If this legibility continued to improve, they could be quite readable by morning.

But again illness and fatique overwhelmed me. I put the sheets back in the case and went to sleep. During the night I experienced more spells of fever accompanied by the sensation of audible but invisible flutterings.

By morning the illness was gone. I awoke with a start when the events of the previous day flooded into my consciousness. Suddenly and brilliantly the sun invaded my room.

I leaped from bed and grabbed my case. Eagerly I tore it open and discovered the strange sheets were still there. The crisp English sentences were bright, sharp, and exquisitely written on a kind of gossamer stationery.

I do not need to comment on the contents of the strange papers, for they formed the document that has become this book. I sensed in my first hurried reading that the material was in the process of decay even as I set about the task of copying it. What I thought I had, I now knew I was about to lose. I grabbed a pad and a pen and began the transcription in a race against time. I was determined that it be a race I would not lose.

I neared the end of my work twenty-four hours later. As I copied the last few pages, they were hard to read, and some of the text was obscure. The characters faded. The sheets grew again transparent and soon were invisible. Shortly even the desk where I had last lain them would not yield a tactile smudge. It was as though they had been absorbed into the wood and were gone.

All that remains from those curious pages is my handwritten copy. It is my hope that the reality of the elusive original will affirm the existence of a world which parallels our own.

The material herein contained was not intended for publication—at least on this planet. I believe I have acted properly, however, in releasing this manuscript. If not, I alone bear the responsibility. I have changed the names of the mortals involved. The other names appear exactly as I found them.

Calvin Miller

Omaha, Nebraska

# To the Committee

I still find it hard to believe that of all the places on the planet that I might have desired, I have managed to arrive in Cleveland. I was in Japan the last time I came here, and I cannot say that I liked it any better than America. Either place is difficult once you have known the great dwellings of our realm. My exploits in Ohio cannot be of much interest to anyone in Upperton. Still, gentlemen, it will be your duty to explore these pages. They contain the tale of Mr. J. B. Considine. In his latter years—though he did not live to be very old—he worked as a junior executive of a firm called International Investors.

He was a baby when we first met. Aren't they all? I did not then suppose his life would hold much interest, and for the twenty-six years I knew him I was torn between compassion and revulsion. He seemed to prefer a lifestyle never founded on anything ideal. Vices rather than virtues claimed his interest. Most of his friends held his same erstwhile appetites and lifestyle. They have a saying in Cleveland that birds of a feather flock together. In J. B.'s case, his feathers matched the flock.

He seldom spoke of God and never in a complimentary fashion. He never even dreamed clean. His priority was himself. Only near the end of his years did he finally achieve anything significant as his life at last turned toward greatness. Unfortunately he did not live long thereafter. The events that led to that strange reversal are all recorded in this report. I must not leave the Committee with the negative notion that I did not love him. I cared for him as God Himself for twenty-six years. But like God, my own ardent love could not motivate him to crave the right.

My short years in Cleveland have taught me many things. At least my previous assignment was an atheist who read much and drank little. Mr. Considine completely reversed these values. An atheist may sometimes live more purposely than a small believer who only drifts between cocktail lounges glutting himself on amusements. My Cleveland assignment taught me that a man may never reject God as a true being, yet live an indulgent life that leaves no place for the Almighty.

If the Committee is prone to be critical of my penchant for summarizing, believe me, it is only in the interest of shortening this document. After my summary of his first twenty-five years, I will deal in detail only with his last year of life. I have recorded these events in the present tense just as they happened.

I do not want to question your administration of the Couriers Elite. If it is at all possible, however, I would like a period of rest before my next assignment. My last two were a bit close together. Is it wise? Should anyone be asked to endure the dull illumination of places like Cleveland and Tokyo too frequently?

I am sure that you will find the report satisfactory, considering that it does end well. If I may be of any help in clarifying this report, please call on me. You can reach me by getting in touch with the Magistrate of Cogdill where I will be residing. I am completing these pages from the bus station in Cleveland. My time is short. I wish I could truthfully say it makes me sad.

Were I human, I would be troubled with the diesel odor from the huge buses. As it is, the odor is not so offensive as the delay. I am comforted but confounded. I shall have to leave the planet by way of a common bus. Since the time is at hand, I will not be negative, though I would have preferred to finish writing this report somewhere other than my lap.

> *Love is light*
> *And best it glows*
> *Where hate is night*
> *And Glory flows.*

Alleluia,

Valiant

 **The Summary**

I smile now when I think of how loudly I once protested this assignment. An American businessman! Not that I ever really wanted to disagree with the High Command. But I find the distance from Upperton to America more than simple galactic flight. And young executives . . . well, they have an interesting piece of office equipment here in Muddyscuttle known as a Xerox copier whose sole virtue is the flawless reproduction of typed trivia. The machine must have been invented by an American businessman desperate to clone his race.

My charge is but a Xerox of all the others. He has no idea that the "brilliant" career he had planned will soon be taken up by someone who also is yet another carbon of himself. If he ever suspected that he was about to leave this corporation through accidental death, he would be terribly troubled. His business is small, but he imagines it to be strategic.

I remember how I early longed to be the guardian of a minister of religion—particularly a zealous evangelical. A Catholic monk would have been even nicer, since it is easy to guard a prayer room and monasteries are as quiet for guardians as for monks. It is never worthwhile looking back, and thinking of what might have been is always the most worthless of pursuits.

On the basis of my youth I hope any hint of impertinence in this report may be forgiven. May this be so especially in the filing room. These past years have left me with greater insecurity than I felt even as a cherub. I may have a touch of angelic dyspepsia, but I assure you, it is not the serious kind. Who can long stand a grumbling angel?

I have never forgotten that Daystar began his Great Insurrection by frowning and skipping his morning Alleluias. It must have seemed minor at the time, but hell grows out of paradise gone sour. Joy is a discipline, and fallen angels were always those who grew negligent with their praise. The air grows frigid when I recall that the pit is deep and dark and cold. There the fire is frozen by frowning angels who once lived in light without smiling.

So I smile! Sometimes I even grin that I have been the guardian of such an aggressive businessman. Oh, how J. B. dreams his young dreams! He constantly pictures himself as the president of the company and flitting in high self-esteem through a universe of secretaries who worship him, fight to take his dictation, carry in his mug of coffee, light his cigars, and make over his ideas. He sits on the edge of his none-too-large desk like Nero in a Kuppenheimer and strokes his chin and talks while the steno pads fill up with letters and memos. He is a winsome bachelor whose beautiful fans applaud his executive future.

His future will be neither as executive nor as long as he now thinks. That's the problem with businessmen. They are forever planning to succeed without any real understanding of what Upperton calls success.

Angelic illusion? Perhaps, for I do remember a certain Reverend Beedle. His angel had a devil of a time of it—if I may mix a metaphor—for Beedle was not so reverend as his parish assumed. His guardian, a certain Sunshade of Glaredill, suffered much with his pastoral hypocrisy. Beedle's species is all too common. (One often hears that ministers of religion run off with choir members or finance excursions with missionary funds.) Beedle was finally locked away in prison. And Sunshade, who tends to like excitement, is sitting out his boring and weary imprisonment. But other than a consecrated monk, what could be easier to guard than a caged cleric? Grimdeeds are minimal under lock and key.

Some Couriers I knew received totemists and shamans for assignments. I sometimes stop and remind myself that there are far more angels assigned to people in other religious systems than there are to the whole of Christendom. My client may not be a lover of the Logos, but at least he does not seek divine guidance by kneeling before totems or reading the digestive systems of slaughtered animals.

I have been pleased that my task is set in Western culture. The West may not be the model for world morality, but in the East there is far less opportunity to learn of Logos love.

And I suppose that remembering my last tour on the planet, I should be grateful to have a client who at least believes in God. Atheism is the great slur in our realm. It is spiritual retardation, but on this planet it flourishes with respect. God-scoffers are the most burdensome sort to care for. I cannot tell you the number of times my last charge cried "nihil" right in my face. He always left me aching over the stubbornness of his own deadly mindset.

It was all so frustrating. I always shielded him from harm while he obstreperously stood against my existence. Yet here was his dark inconsistency. He scoffed at angels, but revered demons, though he never admitted it. He saw demonic and horrendous images swim the wallpaper at midnight. He was terrified both of darkness and of death. Most who curse the High Command lack courage to doubt Daystar. But skeptics may fear the dark and yet put on a courageous show in well-lighted lecture halls.

I loved my former client. The Logos did, too. I worked in that fruitless affection for eighty-six years, until the final day he clutched his throat and went to join Daystar. Instantly, of course, he came to belief, but late faith is unavailing. There's little use accepting arks once the rain begins to fall. Death is such an instant storm that by the time you reach for an umbrella, you already need your water wings.

There is but one rule for angels or men: TRUST. Angels thrive on the principle; very few men ever manage it. To my charge, "trust" is a quantity of capital held in a fund. He believes in trust funds, but has never given the word "trust" any better definition.

I cannot quote our Logos exactly, but His best advice to aggressive executives dreaming of power and corporate influence would probably be, "What shall it profit any company climber if he gains the corporation and loses himself?" And saddest of all is that the business J. B. served in true perspective was a comic mirror where his own ego was but a distorted image of his self-importance.

So I am glad that my sojourn on Muddyscuttle is nearly done. It has been a trifling twenty-six years—shorter than the usual assignment. My youthful charge has just boarded a bus and begun a trip from which he will never return. Typically, he and I entered Muddyscuttle the same year and shall make our exit together. He will "die," as shortsighted Muddyscuttlers say. As they view it, the accident tonight will be the ultimate tragedy. They will grieve the event, mark it with a satin-box ritual, and go home to speak of how natural he looked.

Why do they speak of naturalness at a time like this? They pack their departed in roses and whisper above the organ music of naturalness. Fortunately, neither of us will be here for the memorial services.

And that is what they are called—"Memorial Services." They use these opportunities to call to memory the life and works of "The Dear Departed." In this case my client is "The Dear Departed" and has not done much that is worthy, so there will be little to call to mind.

Still, they will sigh above his flowery finale that he was always a "good egg." Who's to deny it? Eggs are sold by the dozen and indistinguishable from others around them. They are easily scrambled. Once broken, they are never collectible again. To exalt such little deeds may seem preposterous in Upperton, but morality gets collected in little curds down here, and small goodnesses are the most regular forms. So they will remember his infrequent virtues and speak of them with superlative phrases. They will eulogize the egg.

He did, however, just recently achieve something . . . ah, but wait! Let me take the events of his mundane life in order without jamming the end against the first.

I remember my first abrupt meeting with him. I faced Cleveland with reluctance. Atmosphere always takes some getting used to. It is as invisible as we are, only thick and sticky. You feel as though you are always pushing against it. I felt awkward in it, much as these earthlings would feel if they were suddenly forced to live submerged in water. Both sight and movement are possible, but there is a thick resistance that clots the vision and sticks spirit to matter.

So from the light, clean freedom of Cogdill, I found myself in atmosphere, squirming to adjust to materiality. I heard an infant cry! Both the baby and I wriggled to adjust to the same new life at the same instant. We both disliked it, but he screamed and kicked and wept.

Crying is common in this world. It does little good to ask the reason for it. Muddyscuttle is what one might call a weeping planet. Laughter can be heard here and there, but by and large, weeping predominates. With maturity the sound and reason for crying changes, but never does it stop. All infants do it everywhere—even in public. By adulthood most crying is done alone and in the dark.

Weeping, for babies, is a sign of health and evidence that they are alive. Isn't this a chilling omen? Not laughter but tears is the life sign. It leaves *weeping* and *being* synonyms. And this is how it was the night our twenty-six-year relationship began.

I was aware of my invisible brothers about me in the birthing room. It was a dingy comedown from the brightness of Cogdill, even though the room was well-lit when he wriggled into life. There was much excitement about his birth, even as ruddy and clamorous as it was.

May I make a suggestion to you on the Committee: Guardians should have more preparation for the crudity of biology. It is difficult to show up for service on the planet and be doubly shocked by materiality and biology. All the odors and colors of life fluids must be dealt with in the birthing room.

Still, when I saw the weeping infant, I was immediately possessive. Biological though he was, I knew instantly he was mine. I felt the awful burden of responsibility for his well-being. I also knew that he possessed something not permitted to me—a nervous system. He was destined to "hurt." I didn't want him to, but I felt I would not be able to stop him from the pain. I watched as the nurse handled him too roughly. She scrubbed him up while he continued his infernal—if I may use such a word—wailing.

In but a few moments I found my repugnance

for his materiality dissipating. I determined to be the best of all guardians, and I have been by his side the entire twenty-six years. He has never suspected my presence. It is well.

It was three days before he was named. During those days I stood in the nursery of the hospital, never leaving his crib. "It's a boy!" they said. His father gave cigars, which were smoked to celebrate his nativity. I did not understand the smoky ritual of birth. Neither did they, but they puffed and billowed with gusto. (I no longer feel it necessary to delve into the reasons behind human antics. I have discovered that most of their nuances are irrational even to themselves.)

When they finally named him, he was called Johnnie Bertram Considine. While I did not find his name lovely, I could not stem the flow of affection that I felt for him. I was anxious lest the slightest harm should come to him. Mine was the same unmanageable, furious love as comes from the Logos Himself.

It was not as though I did not love other mortals, for I felt attracted to them all. But Johnnie Bertram was the eye of my affection.

Many events in his infancy troubled me. I ached the night he put his hand too quickly in his father's coffee. It hurt him dreadfully, and I found myself angry that they had been so haphazard in caring for him. I wanted him never to be hungry. While we are never permitted to resent humans, I found certain gaps in my good will when his mother let him cry at night because she wished he wouldn't. She put on good shows of affection when her motherhood was on display. But when the 2 A.M. feeding annoyed her, she would let her irritation show by the way she tugged violently on Johnnie's tiny form.

I discovered that I was the very first to be able to communicate with Johnnie. I found that while my spirituality did not form words such as humans do with their material system of speech, I could plant wordless concepts of love and purity into his mind. All this was achieved while he was but a baby. There was a certain spiritual capacity in Johnnie that remained open to my communication.

I remember Pascal's old guardian, Starstone, telling the Couriers Elite about this spiritual capacity. He was fond of quoting the human genius of his charge, who reminded Muddy-scuttlers that there was a god-shaped vacuum in every life which only "God" could fill.

I could make Johnnie smile by these thoughtless suggestions to his inner person. Smiling is ever welcome on a crying planet. And when he smiled, they would gather about his crib and "tickle" him beneath his chin and marvel at his grin as though they had created it. But I knew, and hoped that in time Johnnie's own experience level would tell him sublimi-nally, that I was really the one doing it.

It never happened.

His identity was fixed and yet uncertain. During his first year his father began to call him "Googul," for what reason I will never be sure. During his second year they called him "Bubby." By his third it was "Sonny." But when he started to school they had settled on "J. B.," a name that stuck to him for the remainder of his twenty-six years.

Muddyscuttlers, at least in Ohio, all begin their education as kindergartners. This is a term of German extraction that I believe means "children's garden," though I am not sure. It was about then that I began feeling Johnnie's first attempts to shut me out. Any influence I brought to bear upon him was shrugged aside. He was mischievous, and his parents permissive. They were influenced by the new psychology that sees all forms of spanking as barbaric. Spanking—if the term be unknown to the Committee—is the procedure of inverting

25

children and flailing their fleshy posteriors in the interest of their futures. I lived in close proximity to the guardians of his parents, and I knew they were constantly trying to get his parents to use more discipline in J. B.'s life. The parents rarely yielded. And since his parents were not affording him much direction, I found it hard to get through to him myself.

Guardians know the better world. But there is only one place on Muddyscuttle where our world is addressed, and that is church. The Considines never went. I should say almost never. They did take little Johnnie there at the first of his Googul existence. It was the season when humans baptize their little ones into the faith. Into what faith I was never sure, since the elder Considines had no faith of their own and little esteem for anyone else's. There is a popular cliché down here that rails against "pie in the sky," and Johnnie's father had long ago decided against spoon-feeding his son "sky pie." He had determined to bypass religious training and to rear him with a "realistic" world view.

During Johnnie's seventh year, his father had a business problem that jeopardized his employment. He became remote and irritable. During this time he began to drink more heavily than he "ought to." He was fond of saying it just this way, though he never seemed to make it clear how heavily one ought to drink. The additional financial pressures that came upon the home introduced a marriage crisis that seemed beyond resolution. The volume of their arguments grew intense and left little Johnnie afraid.

I had discovered the principle of pride in Johnnie's life, but it was fledgling and soft compared to that which I saw at work in his parents. Pride is the last-ditch, violent stand of the human ego. It causes men to cling to their rights even when they discover that their rights are clearly wrong. It tries to coerce every other human viewpoint to logic of its own. It knows only how to win.

Both of his parents were proud; thus, they argued. Sometimes when they argued, Mr. Considine would stomp out of the house and slam the door. He would be gone most of the night. When he finally did return, he would stumble up the stoop and fumble for the keyhole. "Drunk" is the shortest colloquialism to describe him. At these times J. B. would retreat to his room and cry.

At such moments I hovered close to my small charge, finding my angelic nature a tremendous disadvantage. He needed the comfort of a flesh and blood physiology, and we guardians lack that blessed curse. Skin stimulation is so affirming to human nervous systems. I craved at these moments the solid incarnation that our Logos once achieved. In human suffering there are times when materiality can serve best.

Angels cannot touch. Let the Committee remember this weakness. It is for this reason that the Logos became a man. During those long and lonely nights with my little charge I learned this great truth. We cannot save what we cannot touch. It was skin that clothed the eternal nature and made our High Command touchable.

What an organic blessing is the simple skin. What confirmation these mortals find in touching each other. Where there is touching, men grow secure and lovers remain in love. Where there is too little of it, frightened children weep at night, and the race grieves.

How I have longed for one square centimeter of skin to set it firm on Johnnie's own! Without it I hovered, useless in his crying nights.

It is Daystar I resent at such moments. He, too, is spirit. But, oh, how he exploits the mortal need for touching to his own ends. He knows that touching given too much license sets sleeping inhibitions free. The whole world then becomes a marketplace for sin, as these mortals call grimdeeds. Johnnie's father broke the vows of marriage to shop this marketplace. The pall of his appetite stretched over Johnnie's own mind and habits.

It started early. When J. B. was only nine he wrote a dreadful word upon the sidewalk in yellow chalk. I pled with him to think the higher words, for men will become their thoughts. Daystar had his way with Johnnie more often than I did, I am afraid. He craved only what his mind imagined.

The problems in his home increased over the next few years. They were never worse than at Christmastide. Mrs. Considine overspent and Mister overdrank. The result was disastrous. On the morning of the anniversary of the Logos' birth, both of them suffered from the results of their indulgence. On those Christmases my charge clung to the toys they bought him, hungry for any evidence of love.

Johnnie was still getting no exposure at all to the church. He had rarely gone since his baptism. With nothing bigger to believe in, he was compelled to believe in himself. Middle-class Muddyscuttlers either learn of the Logos or they learn to survive without Him. Survival is a kind of coping where men play hero to themselves. They bulldoze their way to meaning, and they worship what they hope to become. They have a local hero in this hemisphere who wears blue tights and a red cape and flies faster than a guardian—though they would say speeding bullet. This super Scuttler is the ego extension of the man who makes it on his own. He is a great positivist who leaps tall buildings at a single bound. Most children, including Johnnie, know more about this muscled messiah than they do the Logos.

The years tumbled over one another. In spite of long periods of loneliness, J. B. struggled on with manufactured hope. His infantile insecurity turned in time to adolescent bravado. He was not unnecessarily vicious as a teen-ager, but he was a prankster.

Through all his early years there was only one touch of spiritual hope for the boy . . . Aunt Ida. She was his father's sister, and she came to visit them on many occasions. In her absence the Considines often referred to her as a fanatic, but Johnnie loved her nonetheless. Whereas his father read him fairy tales, Ida read him stories from the Bible. In his early years Johnnie mixed the stories very badly. He could never remember if Rapunzel or Rebecca was Isaac's wife. He was sure that Hansel and Gretel and Jonathan and David played together in the Dark Forest. For J. B. life was special with his auntie, and he always wanted her to stay longer than she did.

She was quaint and unlike the Considines. She was devout. She was what the Muddyscuttle atlas calls a Kentuckian. Her whole personality was warmed by her affection for the Logos, whom she knew and loved in her own way.

She was not able to bring about any real spiritual advances in Johnnie's family, but she touched Johnnie and hugged him right on into his teens. So he was able to discover in her a God that had enough skin to be credible. In fact, as J. B. could understand the Logos at all, he attached the entire definition to Aunt Ida.

She gave him a little Bible for his fourteenth birthday, but he could make no sense of it. Desiring to please her, he set out at once to read it, but became mired in the genealogies of Genesis and laid the book aside. He was never quite able to understand how a book so heavy with long names had ever managed to become the favorite of someone as lovable and touchable as Aunt Ida.

As he neared his sixteenth year, the course of his life was to make a radical change. His mother and daddy's guardians met me in the hall one night in the month of February. They were ready to return to Upperton. I knew they were about to leave Muddyscuttle, and I braced myself for what shortly transpired. The house was quiet, but the silence was like the calm before a storm. It was ominous. The guardians reminded me that this was the final hour that the Considines would be on the Scuttle. They were in grief that J. B.'s parents had never come to know the reclamation which is the single important event toward which all Couriers move their clients. The poor guardians had not succeeded and now were noticeably grieved. They were soon to be separated from their charges forever.

I must say that I have rarely seen such glum guardians. The Logos during His sojourn here referred to humans without hope as "the lost." The term fits in so many ways. It seems to me that during their lifetimes Johnnie's parents were lost. Lost to all they were, to what they might have been. Psychologically lost, lost to love, to destiny. But worst of all, they were lost to the Logos and His all-important presence— the presence without which all is absence. Having all their lives known only His absence, they were soon to discover that the very composition of their destiny was absence.

But let me not interrupt my story. While I meditated upon the morose Couriers, I realized that the hallway was filling with smoke. Knowing that humans can stand very little of the vaporous substance, I ran to Johnnie's room and moved through his conscience. He was instantly awake. I led. Unseeing, he never knew why he followed, but follow he did, till he was safe outside.

The fire began in his parents' bedroom. Johnnie tried to rush back into the house and call them to safety, but the flames were too intense.

Firemen found him wandering aimlessly

on the lawn before his home. Though he was in his teens, he was clutching tightly to a teddy bear that Aunt Ida had given him on a long-forgotten Christmas. For some reason his hands, flailing in the darkness, had touched the stuffed animal, and he had dragged it from his home, which was shortly incinerated. The bear never left his bedroom for the remainder of his life. He did have some trouble explaining it to his college fraternity, but he kept it. It was to him a strong symbol of survival. It may sound strange in Upperton, but it became to him a theological icon. The Bible Aunt Ida had given him perished in the fire. But the bear had drawn him to life.

Grief in adolescence is a folding of the soul. Never have I seen a mortal grieve as he did. Never have I wanted anything more than to have the power of touch. But my shortcoming was redeemed by the kind Kentuckian. Ida was there and held him through the many hours that he waited for the satin-box ritual.

Johnnie had little to move since everything was lost in the fire. He went back to Kentucky with Aunt Ida and Uncle Harvey. Uncle Harvey will need no special reference. He was not well and died shortly after J. B. arrived. His death left his widow in a kind of ache which J. B. in his own grief helped to heal.

He thought to attend church with Aunt Ida, but the sermons were too long and the music too slow. He openly declared after a couple of months that church, like the Bible, was all right for Aunt Ida but not for him. My hopes for J. B.'s reclamation degenerated rapidly over the next few years. I still did my best to encourage him toward morality and straight thinking, but such items were not high on his priorities any more. His years in the college fraternity further loosened his idealism. From college he "knocked about" for a couple of years before he finished his masters degree in business. It was a mundane but typical course of Muddyscuttle study.

I hope the Committee will not think this summary too terse. I feel I have given those years more time and detail than they deserve. So let us proceed directly to the beginning of J. B.'s twenty-fifth year. While I have summarized his early years, I am leaving the final part of this document exactly as I wrote it. The final year of his life is the one that holds the significance for which reports like this are written.

It will sound odd to speak in Upperton of his final year, for there are no final years.

> *Tell all the mighty ones, truth does not lie*
> *Where trumpets have sounded the news.*
> *The Logos sleeps warm in the womb of the*
>   *sky,*
> *Yet weeps before men without shoes.*

Alleluia,

Valiant

Friday,
June 25

International Investors held a dinner in J. B.'s honor because he was new to the firm. Now, I am afraid, he is comatose and inebriated. I have not struggled this hard in my eternal life. Even before dinner I realized that he had already had too much to drink. Temperance has never appealed to J. B.; the ghost of his father lives on. Everytime J. B. went back to the bar, I urged him away. His intemperance fires him with a chemical courage toward the opposite sex.

Three times he tried to set up a comfy session at his apartment after dinner. Thankfully, none of those whom he propositioned were open to his suggestions. His intentions were not honorable, but they are customary in Cleveland. The base things he had in mind would beggar the fallen angels. At such moments I cherish my lost dream of having as my charge a well-behaved cleric or even an honorable layman. But being realistic, I accept life as it has been given to me to deal with.

After all these years I still experience materiality shock. Knowing that I have only a little time left to endure my assignment helps me adjust to the burdens of this realm. Observing people, I have come to understand the exact nature of the sacrifice of the Logos. It was not so much dying as a man but becoming one that was the sacrifice. Materiality is a prison of flesh which the fleshly enjoy. How much my client enjoys his captivity!

Such captivity is shattered by reclamation, for the Logos is a powerful force for self-control. Oh, how J. B. needs such a force! Here is but a little list of his misdemeanors for a couple of hours:

6:00 P.M.	He purchased an unsavory magazine from a newsstand. I'm not sure even the Lord High Command knows of this one.
6:15 P.M.	He used the name of the Lord High Command in a Muddy-scuttle phrase.
6:20 P.M.	He lusted after a girl at a crosswalk while I tried to get his mind on a business proposition. Perhaps the Committee will object that I did not try to get his mind directly on the Logos. Such a proposition is now so remote to my client that it would not be possible.
7:00 P.M.	He lusted after a picture of a girl who appeared in the magazine he bought at six o'clock. I tried to get him to read *Popular Mechanics* instead.
8:00 P.M.	He lusted after one of the secretaries at the dinner held in his honor.

This brief cataloging illustrates my forebodings. J. B.'s greatest interests are my greatest fears. He is preoccupied with sex. What a three-letter spoiler is this little word. It fills his mind constantly with images of full indulgence. He has but to view a strand of hair or a free ankle and he can build intense intrigues and fiery fantasies.

These, of course, did not begin at the party. In the summary I could have mentioned that by the time he was fourteen he had an imagination that was adequate to spark an inferno. This wanton madness of his has grown across the years. He might curtail it by taking some charge of his mind and thus avoid the storms of unrequited desire that come completely to a calm only when his appetite has fed.

Usually he lives between longings and guilt. He seeks to cool the fever of his passion in indulgence. When he does indulge, he suffers. After his indulgence, guilt is so grievous he can barely be cordial to those who afford him the pleasure.

And how does guilt stalk him? His fiery sexual visions are immediately replaced by a vision of Aunt Ida wagging her head and shaking her finger at him. At such moments he cannot even stand to look at the teddy bear he still keeps in his bedroom. Ever since the night it saved him from the fire he has had a strange desire to honor it with a high morality he dare not dwell upon.

Human ecstasy and guilt are born in one seething—full, yet empty—moment. To think that this reckless force was given so that Adam and his mate might not be too casual in populating the empty planet! J. B. wants all of Adam's ecstasy and none of his responsibility. He has never considered sex as the work of the Divine Creator for anything so practical as "replenishing the earth." Sex is for himself. So much so that most of his consorts are not persons but commodities.

I wonder how long he can go on using women before he loves one. Will he ever come to that place where love replaces transaction? Now all is for himself: the geography, the time, the great orchestras that play through muted speakers, the flowers, the wine, the perfume, the softness and violence—all serve nothing but his own nervous system.

J. B. calls this "tea for two." But he is after the whole teapot. He consumes it all for himself. At the height of his indulgence there are not two. There is only he—narcissus, fondling his own manhood, breathing heavily over his own desirability. Pretending to be sharing, he grabs all delight and crams it into his own knapsack.

His behavior at the party was consistent with his life as a whole. I felt a comradeship in watching the other guardians there. The whole lot of us were scurrying about in an attempt to keep grimdeeds at a minimum. But it was a maximum night.

The only guardian I envied was Cloudsong. His charge is a posh assignment: a certain John McDonald who is a teetotaling fundamentalist. Cloudsong was a little arrogant about his client's exemplary behavior. He was the only angel who had time to sit in the corner and catch up on writing his report. McDonald left at 10:30—hardly the hour that the "red-blooded" depart—and probably both he and Cloudsong were at rest before midnight. The boss confided to J. B. that McDonald was a "Seven-Up sipper" and hence is called a fuddy-duddy throughout the company.

But whatever his reputation at International Investors, McDonald has left Cloudsong the envy of the angels. I am almost to change my mind about clerics being the easy ones. I think I would rather have a fundamentalist fuddy-duddy—especially a married fuddy-duddy. Mrs. McDonald has a certain pinched look that must have been of some assistance to Cloudsong. Even a fundamentalist who would defy his guardian might not have the courage to go against a countenance like that.

J. B. is across the gamut from John McDonald. J. B. neither resists nor struggles against booze or lust. His morality comes from his monolithic view of his world. The world is one. It is all matter. His real barrier to achieving a quality life is that he cannot imagine any other form of reality. Sex and liquor can both be touched. They form a grotesque image of what is real. Materialism is the ultimate barrier to faith. Because of it men admire the stuff of existence rather than existence itself.

Sexuality has been made the great good on Muddyscuttle. Fie upon this evaluation! Woe to all who so perceive it! I remember at all J. B.'s parties that some of the guardians recorded in the Book once tried to enter the field of human sexuality and were given up to Daystar's chains. It is hard to believe angels would stoop so low. They should not have looked. Lust is always born in sight. What can be seen may be craved. Still, I cannot fathom how McDonald manages to avoid what is so desired by all the others.

I am not sure that things are as they appear / see p. 38 para. 2 with John McDonald. I know his guardian well. We once served the Couriers Elite in Muddyscuttle's Eastern Hemisphere together. I am suspicious that Cloudsong knows that McDonald is what our Logos called a hypocrite during the painful years he spent in these wallows. McDonald's prayers have only an eighty-foot radius. His low-wattage communication is as infrequent as it is weak. Religion is a show and not a way of life with him.

Cloudsong told me McDonald only really prayed once. His only prayer to make it all the way to Human Petitions was the one he uttered the night he lost control of his Pontiac on a mountain road. His bumper caught on a tree stump, and Upperton has not heard from him since. Cloudsong probably has no fewer problems than other guardians—they are only different in nature.

Seeing Cloudsong with his new charge has

left me in a quandary. I can't decide whether I had rather guard a lecher or a hypocrite. There is an unpleasant odor in McDonald's sanctity. His piety too soon congratulates itself. But at least he is headed for Upperton. J. B.'s heading is not so fortuitous at the moment.

Every time J. B. swears, which is frequent, McDonald smugly rejoices over his own moderate speech. Cloudsong does warn him against such smugness, but nothing preempts his self-righteousness. Once when J. B. told an off-color story, McDonald left the lounge indignant that there were overtones of grimdeeds in my client's life.

McDonald is full of God-talk when it is convenient and when it is not. He has invited J. B. to church with him this weekend, and I can only hope he will go. He finds a kind of Aunt-Ida fascination with McDonald's "Holy-Roller mentality." There is some possibility he will go, especially if he thinks he might catch sight of some "religious chickie." With this term J. B. must certainly refer to those women Mr. McDonald would call his sisters in Jesus.

I would not leave the impression with the Committee that I believe that there are only two grimdeeds, nor even that grimdeeds consist more of action than thought. The great grimdeeds of every era are sociological, to be sure. Man's inhumanity to man: these are the great grimdeeds of genocide, racism, and unbridled power. I will not fall error to the same mistaken values that have plagued the church in other ages. How often has the church crusaded against booze and loose women, but never found the time or courage to address the great woes that leave the cities thronged with refugees from hope.

Still, J. B. is not so wide a thinker as to see these larger grimdeeds. His is a near-sighted hedonism that might be called the "Whisky and Women" syndrome.

Now the party is over, and I am trying not to dwell on the length of my assignment. I am taking it one day at a time. Methuselah's old guardian, Featherdraggle, used to say that no matter how tough it gets in the material realm, be grateful that Logos has put a limit on human existence. The whole thing will be over in seventy years. At least this is the average. I take heart in remembering that what Featherdraggle had to endure for centuries will soon be over for me.

> *Alleluia and praise to the Lord High Command*
> *With Nova-blue Starfire encircling His head.*
> *He holds constellations with wounds in those hands,*
> *Now breaking the light-years—once breaking the bread.*

Alleluia,

Valiant

Monday,
June 28

Things are sweet and sour at once.

What could be better than a Muddyscuttle summer day?

Considine did go to church yesterday, but he told a friend in his carpool this morning, "I don't think I want in on this religious jag." Church offended him. Having lived through it with him, I think his honesty may be on the side of the angels.

We have been to church so seldom that I had forgotten the obscenity of some Muddyscuttle worship. I was stunned at the starkness of human praise in this particular service. The singing was more Hallelujah than Alleluia; Upperton became "Up yonder." Humans called ushers met the guests at the door to help them find a seat. I couldn't understand this, since so many were empty and no one would have had the slightest difficulty finding one.

These ushers also gave worshipers a bulletin. This paper had the order of worship all printed out along with the church softball and bowling schedules for the week. It was a most unusual document. It also contained advice to pray for the sick so that they could soon be back in worship. I could not escape the feeling that the sick may not want back in.

The service began as the choir entered and sang. I have heard few choirs since I left Upperton, but I was shocked at what tonsils and adenoids do to praise. J. B., unaccustomed to anything finer, was not offended at this. After the choir sang, there was a period of general singing called "congregational hymns." J. B. had some trouble with this. They sang a hymn called "Come Thou Fount." He was a little embarrassed that he had no idea what a Fount was, but he assumed it was because he was so irregular at church. The second verse had an entreaty to "build an Ebenezer"; J. B. felt it must be at least as hard to sing about Ebenezers as it would be to construct one.

John McDonald seemed to enjoy everything. Not so his guardian. My assessment of McDonald is correct. Cloudsong has urged McDonald to lower the volume of his singing, for he was always louder than the rest. During the sermon Cloudsong could not keep his charge awake. He spent the entire service seeking either to silence or to rouse his client.

During the offering J. B. put in two little green pieces of paper currency called "bucks" and smiled at his generosity and sacrifice. I tried to keep him from feeling self-righteous, but he grew smug. His religious arrogance lasted only until the man down the pew put in twenty bucks. Then J. B. looked down and was clearly glad when the offering was over.

They had a special soloist who was listed in the bulletin as "Gloria and Her Gospel Guitar." She strummed and sang the most unusual piece of music I have ever heard. The song was called "I'm Just a Jesus Cowgirl on That Trail to the Sky." I thought her song was satire and was really enjoying it until I noticed several Scuttlers around me crying from the emotional impact. *Gloria* is a favorite word in Upperton anthems, so I was expecting something a little more *in excelsis deo*. But this Gloria was not in the *excelsis* category.

Her second selection was entitled "Life Is Like a Mountain Railway." It was loaded with lyrical advice to "keep yer hand 'pon the throttle an' yer eye 'pon the rail." The song was filled with railroad imagery and seemed to speak of the Logos in a brakeman's cap. Before long, Brother Buford, a good Kentuckian, got up to preach. His congregation listened intently, but his dialect never translated. Nor did his message.

I'm afraid it may take a good deal of effort to get J. B. back to church again.

I was troubled by the kind and quality of worship in the church. I know I must not berate the sincere, whatever their level of excellence. Still, I wonder how some of these poor Scuttlers will ever stand the transition to Upperton. They have a condition down here known as culture shock. Scuttlers often experience it when they move from one country to another. But I can barely imagine the shock that Upperton will be to all these materialists. How shall these who find worship in this sort of praise ever adjust?

When the sermon and the service ended, the choir sang "God Be With You Till We Meet Again." The implication of the chummy anthem was that He had been there all through the service.

I managed to talk with Cloudsong after the experience. He agreed that there had to be something more effective to motivate J. B. toward reclamation. Cloudsong told me that there is to be a gospel telecast on Thursday. Unfortunately it is across the network from a football game. There is not much chance that J. B. will miss the game.

There is a new man at work whom J. B. has noticed praying in the cafeteria before his meals. To J. B. this is an eccentric and fanatic custom.

The name of the new man is Beau Ridley. He has taken a position in the Corporate Investment Division of International Investors. J. B. has already mentally labeled him a Christian of McDonald's ilk. I earnestly hope that Ridley knows the Logos. His guardian is a certain Joymore, and he appears to be consistently calm. This is a positive quality that may help J. B. to be reclaimed.

My desire to see him "saved," as McDonald would say, is not based upon his moral condition alone. There are many noble things about J. B.'s world view. He loves children and is even considering giving some of his Saturday time to working in a boys' organization in a deprived section of inner Cleveland.

And he is courteous to a fault. He goes out of his way to offer little courtesies to all he meets. He is generous in most every expression of his life. As I said earlier, he has not yet managed to do much thinking about the great injustices of the planet. But were he to take the time for it, I assure you, he would grieve over all he saw once he looked beyond the narrow limits of his world view.

Still, he must be reclaimed, for Daystar's chamber is for ever. I love J. B. too much to let him slip beyond the glorious destiny I have in mind for him.

> Come gallant and glorious, you couriers of
>   love.
> Stir up in your zeal His mighty attack.
> Stand mute for the day that He entered in
>   time.
> Shout songs for the day He came back.

Alleluia,
Valiant

 # A Certain Wednesday in July

I must hurry my client down the pathway to encounter. He is so confident of time that he assumes it is endless. Men do not manage time; time is the manager. Life is short on Muddyscuttle. I knew an old starclerk in Cogdill who used to say, "It seems that I barely get the file folder out of the birth box before I put it back in the death box. There is nothing after that but to put it in hold for the Termination Event."

The most dreaded aspect of human existence is its temporary status. During His humanization the Logos taught "many are called and few are chosen." Sometimes when the wind blows over the planet you can hear humans wail—Muddyscuttlers weeping as they terminate. Only guardians hear it. Yet, it must float to the very foundations of Upperton. How bleak to hear them going off to Daystar's chamber. Guardians are too much enthralled with true life ever to understand the death of the unreclaimed. Everything is so final. We must pull the file, stamp it "Unclaimed," and leave them to their never-finished process of vanishing away.

How opposite is life in Upperton. There

being ever grows and spirits densify and enlarge. How can we know the pain of atrophy, the great curse of decaying materiality? Being, as it withers, ever passing, never gone. Thus, I must work to see if one day I can finally write J. B.'s own name in the Life Book. I constantly think of nothing else. I squint in the dim illumination of this world and carry for him more brilliant hope than he can imagine. I wish J. B. could know that the lighting here is always bad. In time I may learn to love it as much as our Logos did. It is for J. B. alone that I endure his planet with a squinting resentment.

I remember the story they often tell in Upperton. The Lord High Command stepped out in darkness and commanded light to be. How gloriously did the unborn light obey. Born without conception, this swift radiance of Upperton split the void. I am still struck that the German, Albert, understood that light and substance are related in some way. I don't understand the relationship between these two, but I am discovering daily the relationship between light and reality. Let all who read this report understand, reality retreats from darkness. They cancel each other out. It amazes me how Scuttlers are prone to think they know it all, yet live on this dingy planet quarreling over trifles. Their dark love of things in the incandescence of God's reality is ultimately unforgivable.

They spend their years squinting over bankbooks and investments to gain a little gold that paves the streets of Upperton. The treasures of kings are the cobblestones in higher worlds. The prisons here are filled with those who stole but little nuggets of our pavement.

Like other gold-gluttons, J. B. is captive. His appetite for things does not compare with his lust for sex, but they are alike in fervor. He seeks to sate both tastes. Nothing holds such sway above J. B. as these two glistening enticements.

Let me not rail too severely on either the depravity of my client or the material world—which is the only one he has known. Sexuality can be noble in spite of his frequent abuse of it. So can the whole realm of things created.

Still, I remember Muddyscuttle materialists from my tour in the late seventeen hundreds. It was not a long stay, but in the interim I have seen these appetites swell to their current fever. Now idealism has degenerated in the race until every man is a bargain-hunter seeking treasures in shop windows. Each seeks to get the "most stuff" for the smallest price. It all reminds me of a noble Scuttler named Wordsworth who once indicted his race with a sonnet:

> The world is too much with us; late and soon,
> Getting and spending, we lay waste our powers.

Once free of shopping and the bedroom, J. B. would have better light. While his hungers are earthbound, he must content himself with darkness. The light is better when our tastes are higher.

> *The Logos was life but they murdered Him*
> * there*
> *On the planet of crosses and graves.*
> *Love strangles and chokes in the dark, foetid*
> * air*
> *Where men gloat on treasures and rave.*

Alleluia,
Valiant

 **Of August and Two Television Episodes**

A kind of hope occupies my attention.

On an August Sunday J. B. woke up to listen to Carlton Classie, a phenomenon in the "video church." Dr. Classie preaches with a distinct diction and is always very positive about the future of Muddyscuttle and Muddyscuttlers themselves.

This Sunday he delivered a sermon entitled "The Winner." "You can be a winner if you think you are a winner," cried Dr. Classie. J. B. really liked the sermon. His eyes were glued to the TV screen. He moved only once and then in a mummified fashion to the refrigerator to get himself a can of beer.

"Remember," said Classie, "your mentality is your vitality. You can win if your mind doesn't sin. Think high, young man. Your career will soar only where your mind has already flown. God is a flags-down-throttles-open God. Low thinking will never let your career lift off the runway." (Perhaps I will have time later to explain *runway* to the Committee.)

J. B. moved a little closer, lit a cigarette, and snapped the ring on his beer can. "You know, you're right," said J. B. talking abstractly to Dr. Classie, who never stopped.

"God wants winners in this world. No loser ever glorified God. God's mind is so glorious the entire universe proceeded from it. He is the Master Thinker and the Master Mind. If you want to learn to think like God, you must think big! Take those difficulties that threaten you with defeat and wrap them in smiles and give them all back to the Master Mind. Remember the airliner that flies too low is in danger—it is only safe at the heights. Most air tragedies are not *air* tragedies. They occur on the ground. They are runway failures. Lift up to the pure, clear air. There you are alone with perspective. All your little difficulties will dwindle as you gain elevation. Break the grind with a godly mind. Soar. Unchain your soul and take control. Soar . . . Soar . . . SOAR!"

All too soon Dr. Classie's sermon was over. It was the first J. B. ever heard to its conclusion. He belched—like a common runway failure. He reached for his toothbrush just as Dr. Classie swelled gallantly, and he moved in close to the screen saying, "This is Dr. Carlton Classie reminding you to turn your pain to gain. . . . *You* can win if you think you can." The music swelled, and there were some nature photographs. J. B. belched again and turned off the set.

Television is new since my last tour.

How shall I describe TV? It is the monumental preoccupation of the bored. Americans watch an endless parade of video dramas until a million pointless plots have fused. The nation is at peace, and since they will not learn to talk, they watch—obesity with eyeballs. They eat, drink, and make merry all before the video glare. They show little emotion unless there is a power failure. The eighth wonder of the world! How can I tell the Committee of these planetlings so fascinated by a window box of little people? Some sing, some dance, some speak

like Carlton Classie. All across this land a million little people dance to distant signals. The device is the god of secular thralldom. Dr. Classie's is one of the few programs that even hints of Upperton.

A most unusual thing happened on Thursday. J. B. actually watched a gospel telecast. He had intended to watch a sporting event, but as it happened, there was a great deal of video "fuzz" on Channel Three, so football was out of the question. J. B. tried to eliminate the blur. He twisted and adjusted the various knobs of the apparatus in an appeal to clarity. But clarity was not to be his. Finally in utter frustration he spun the channel selector in anger. He left the TV, walked to the bar, and fixed himself a highball.

Channel Six, where the hapless device became fixed, was coming in loud and clear. As he sat down, J. B. faced a stadium filled with people come to listen to a man named Frankie Williams. Before he spoke, the Conquest Choir was singing melodies about sin and eternal life. *I know I must be adjusting to the planet. Perhaps I am overadjusting. I suddenly found myself listening to Frankie Williams just as if I needed what he was saying.*

Best of all, J. B. actually listened to me. When he was about to mix himself a second drink, I suggested that he couldn't afford a moment away from the seat. He shrugged off my initial suggestion, until I reminded him that his Aunt Ida had always admired him and would be embarrassed to know he was drinking in front of a man of God.

Williams was preaching on the Second Coming of the Logos. He preached on human drunkenness and gluttony that would exist at the end of time. At the mention of these intemperances, J. B. sucked in his stomach, covered the candy dish, and pushed his empty cocktail glass out of sight. He fidgeted in his chair. He tried to think about his Aunt Ida. Her image for him was more accessible than the abstract God that Frankie Williams preached.

Then Williams talked about the millions of businessmen in the American corporations who were living for themselves. "These men," he said, "have never really considered making Christ the Lord of their lives." J. B. was actually smitten when the Conquest Choir began singing the entreaty. He was choked with emotion. I thought for a moment he was going to respond when they began to sing:

> Come now unto Jesus, you stained by your sin,
> Full-bathed in His glory, new life may begin.

He turned off the television and went to sit down and breathed deeply. He sighed in relief that the telecast was over.

I prodded him to read the Bible that his Aunt Ida had given him at high school graduation to replace the one burned in the fire. He lifted it from the bookshelf, turned it over in his hand, and began cautiously. Haplessly he thumbed the pages to Matthew One. They all feel they must begin either in Matthew One or Genesis One. "No!" I screamed to his subconscious. "A thousand times no! . . . You'll be right back in the 'begats' again." But he continued, "Zorobabel begat Abiud; and Abiud begat Eliakim."

"I must read on just like Frankie Williams said," he thought. Fighting the urge to quit, he went forward: "Eliakim begat Azor," said Aunt Ida's great gift.

"I wonder why Auntie considered this such a hot gift," he said. "She always said it would bring me comfort in a time of grief. . . . 'Azor begat Sadoc; and Sadoc begat Achim.' And what could she mean that I would find great peace in my conflict? . . . 'Eliud begat Eleazar; and Eleazar begat Matthan.' Some comfort and peace that is," he said, folding the volume.

I urged him to go forward just a little, but he would have none of it. He was utterly bewildered that Aunt Ida and Dr. Classie and Frankie Williams all found such comfort in a book so filled with "begats."

Suddenly I reminded him of one of Auntie's old pastors who always preached by the Index Method. He would close his eyes and open the Bible and put his index finger blindly upon some text and then open his eyes and begin to preach. I know the Committee will think me mad, and I do confess that it was a wild attempt, but let my examiners remind themselves of the desperation I felt as J. B. emerged from the begat passages. He tried the Index Method.

"Oh, God, guide my finger to Thy Word," he said. He felt good about saying "Thy" instead of "Your"; Aunt Ida always said "Thy." With that, he lifted his hand in the air and closed his eyes. He opened his Bible rather near the front and laid his finger on the page. He was astounded as he finally opened his eyes and they fell on the passage just above his index finger.

> Nevertheless these shall ye not eat of them that chew the cud, or of them that divide the hoof: as the camel, because he cheweth the cud, but divideth not the hoof; he is unclean unto you.

"Good advice," thought J. B. "Never eat a camel."

> And the coney, because he cheweth the cud, but divideth not the hoof; he is unclean unto you.

"I need peace," thought J. B. "Can I find it in the Good Book? I must try. I will go on."

> And the swine, though he divide the hoof, and be cloven-footed yet he cheweth not the cud; he is unclean to you. Of their flesh shall ye not eat, and their carcase shall ye not touch; they are unclean to you. These shall ye eat of all that are in the waters: whatsoever hath fins and scales in the waters . . .

55

He continued on for five minutes or so, and then closed the volume. He was not convinced that the index method could ever bring him any of the same esteem for the Scriptures that his Auntie's old minister so enjoyed. He concluded them all to be a kind of third sex. How could anyone find comfort in the Bible: Williams, Classie, Auntie, or the old index-method preacher?

He felt exhausted at his magnificent attempt to read the Bible.

He lay down for his nap.

He might have fallen right off to sleep, but I prevented it by filling his mind with images. I kept playing pictures of his Aunt Ida at prayer across the inner screen of his thoughts. He seemed to be envisioning a change for himself. He was experiencing a destitution—the kind that might actually precede the human phenomenon of repentance. Surely his reclamation will be forthcoming. The starclerk may very soon lift his folder from the file.

> *There is a strand of scarlet fire*
> *That can illuminate the day*
> *And men may warm their dead desire*
> *And crave a life one world away.*

Alleluia,
Valiant

The Trees

The trees are lovely. I am captive to the planet. This bondage fell upon me as I walked with J. B. in the park today. He sat beneath an oak whose tonnage nature had made in a hundred and fifty years. While he wondered over all the years it took to make such a plant, I marveled that it grew so quickly. Oaks are marvels in a topsy-turvy world where trees outlive men.

The groves are grand, but I have heard that in the West there are trees that were already tall when our Beloved walked here. Oh, you Couriers of the Distant Council, I see increasingly why our great Logos loved this planet so! Here the eyes may feast on nature, beholding geese set against the incendiary skies of summer evenings. There are gray mushrooms tufted in ochre grass. J. B. studied a ladybug that walked a spotted-amber promenade upon a linden twig. Does it seem incongruous that angelic eyes would gaze upon an orange insect in admiration for the jewellike precision in the Lord High Command's meticulous detail?

I'm glad J. B. does love nature. I wonder that he remains so free from nature's Maker. J. B. is evidence that creation may stop men short of the Creator. They fondle the art, but never know the Artist. They see a tree and marvel at its beauty, but never go on in logic to the Person their reason should lead them to.

So my charge does not suspect that his awe is only pantheism. He clings so desperately to this world that he cannot even consider the world to come. He is so bound up in his affection for verdant towers and leafy shrines, yet cannot see that his love for nature keeps his altar too low. This leaves not only his life but his destiny earthbound.

Life for J. B. is all too sensual. If he cannot smell it or touch it, it holds no value for him. He walks by all extrasensual reality never suspecting its existence. The same is true for all of these planetlings. Life is comfortable in Cleveland, and none are under any threat of death. This leaves the natural world immediate and ours remote. The martyrs could not afford the luxury of J. B.'s pantheism. They longed for Upperton, for they were about to lose this present world. But in Ohio there are few dangers, so men think they are immortal, and J. B. is among those whose freedom from fear builds pantheistic altars in groves of great oaks.

But I am fickle.

Just when I want to criticize J. B.'s intrigue with the out-of-doors, I become fascinated with a swan moving silently across a pond. September is magnificent and must deserve some little Alleluia. Lest you think I have been distracted from my task by nature, let me assure you my motives are unchanged. I spend every hour now in hope of my client's reclamation.

It is true that I did not fare well in getting him to read his Bible, but I am learning to take one step at a time. I regret that it is forbidden for guardians to have the knowledge of when or if reclamation will occur. Without this information, I remain troubled by the certain event of his termination, which date I do know. There

are only a few more months till his satin-box ritual.

Contemplating the oak tree which he considered old and I young has led me to realize that time is the great scourge of all Scuttlers. I woke myself from my distraction in the park by singing the old guardian air:

> Struggle Couriers and wait
> For every human hour is late,
> And even infants bang death's gate
> Demanding that it open.

Besides my preoccupation with time, I feel that I have become too familiar with Considine. I am his guardian, not his "chum." I realized too late that I almost considered the trip to church and the carpool conversations as outings for the both of us. Our aloneness with the trees was almost rapturous. I was prone to view the telecast with J. B. as a sort of "lovely evening at home." I am trying to remember that I am not on Muddyscuttle upon some sort of interplanetary lark. Time itself should concern me only when I remember it is of utmost importance to him. He will shortly be out of it. I must force myself to remember Raphael's Code, to which I first subscribed my allegiance to Upperton:

> I, Valiant, in the name and authority of the Lord High Command do swear to the beloved Logos, Ruler of spirit and matter, this twofold commission of His Majesty, the only true Sovereign and source of being. First, I shall do all within my power to work with human willfulness so that no unclaimed spirit ever shall be lost in Daystar's prison house of fire. Second, I will guard the physical life of my charge so he may acquire unending life and come with all Upperton to adore the Logos.

It is an unfortunate tendency of guardians to seek friendship with clients. While I am generally doing the right things, I wonder if I am always doing them for the right reasons.

I am spellbound by Frankie Williams. He certainly seems a good ambassador of Upperton. With every Conquest many more come to be listed in the Logos' Book. Some of the planetlings are discovering the sheer delight of the sovereignty of the High Command over their affairs. Upperton ever yearns for the reclamation of this little ball, and the Redemption Carolers are busy, I am sure, praising the liberation of thousands of Muddyscuttlers during every Conquest.

But the Logos never liberates thousands. He always liberates one Muddyscuttler at a time. I must remember that J. B. is in every sense the Logos' charge as he is mine. I must not crowd the Logos' work, but join Him in the effort that is His. We do, indeed, have the same hope and goal.

I no longer feel any envy over Cloudsong's assignment. I should despise to be the guardian of a fundamentalist. McDonald speaks of the Logos while retaining so much fidelity to his own image and his need for recognition. How easily religion may sour! For Cloudsong's client, the church is a miracle show where he beholds nothing of God—only his own goodness! He assumes that God has joined his team and left him the lucky captain.

McDonald grieves because my client is "unsaved," and Cloudsong grieves because his is "too much saved." McDonald's view of the Logos makes God a great "grench" who lords it over humankind for the sheer joy of slapping hands.

It is such a long way between what J. B. is and what McDonald would like him to become. McDonald would like for J. B. to be a Christian rather like himself, since he considers his own faith to be the standard of the planet. If McDonald could only get one glimpse of J. B. sitting in his underclothes with a can of beer in his hand, smoking cigarettes, he would think it impossible for him ever to attain the same level of sainthood he has already achieved. As McDonald sees it, God will drub a man to hell for parlor games, tobacco, or wine.

McDonald has been in constant misery since his reclamation. He suffers from either his guilt of grimdeeds committed or the gnawing fear that he may soon fall into a major grimdeed of some sort. Religious guilt is a violence that obscures God with an egotistic inner focus that produces nothing of value. It steeps in self-concern, and soon everything becomes a passionate preoccupation with the self.

Joymore, an old acquaintance of mine, is the guardian of Beau Ridley, the new man in the company. Ridley is pleasant and forceful, and J. B. is drawn by his charm and wit. J. B. has come to know him and is no longer as critical of Beau as he once was. Most of J. B.'s judgments are *a priori* and therefore, much of the time, wrong. Except for Beau's habit of saying grace in the company cafeteria, which still offends J. B., he is possessed of an authentic masculinity.

As J. B. is drawn to Beau, so also I am to his guardian. I only hope that J. B. and Beau might become friends. This would permit Joymore and me to renew our acquaintance. I used to visit with him regularly several anguria before the humanization of the Logos. A new friendship with someone from home might permit me to escape the earth fever that has captured me of late.

I am an angel in doubt. Maybe it's because my time is short, but my fascination with Muddyscuttle pervades my whole world view. I must be honest: I do love the world where I now serve. I sometimes grieve that the whole planet is destined for fiery erasure at Operation Clockstop. I must redouble my efforts at protecting my charge, lest the ancient fire fall upon him unaware.

62

He is glorious evermore
Who holds both love and fire in store.
Hail the agent of all grace,
The spirit monolith in space!

Alleluia,

Valiant

 # From a Bedroom on an Autumn Night

J. B.'s security is my passion. How shall I really protect my client in such an unpredictable world? There are many things over which I have too little control. The air tragedy but Thursday is an example of what I mean. What if J. B. had been on that plane? All 119 Muddy-scuttlers were "lost," as they say down here. On the same plane there were 119 guardians, never mentioned by the press. It is just as well. None of the guardians could do a thing to avert the disaster.

The fault lies in protoplasm. I am afraid it is so fragile it is not worth its carbon formula. If human flesh goes over a mere 108 degrees, it succumbs to fever; the mind fries and life is gone. If the temperature lowers to 90 degrees, the body dies. Mine is the task of keeping a fragile human being alive until he can be reclaimed. I must make every tragedy a triumph. In every mishap J. B. must be a "survivor." His hope of Upperton means he must remain in the flesh. The flesh—the sinew of dust! What can be said for it? Weather stings it. Sharp objects puncture it. Disease infects it. Old age alone will crack and consume it. Wars liquidate it.

Human beings seem to willfully complicate our work—it is as if they are eager to kill themselves. They assassinate, murder, and declare war. How can we possibly help them stay safe while they dream up a ghastly arsenal of ideas to kill themselves? They dare to set flesh against gunpowder and nuclear fission and war. Nineteen million men die every century from the scourge of this senseless international killing.

I often think of the twenty thousand who died in the planet quake of Anguria Seventeen. Count the combined concern of these twenty thousand guardians who were powerless to stop the carnage. I could go on to speak of such human foibles as the Hindenburg or the Titanic. Specific instances matter not. The point is that again and again Muddyscuttlers have perished by the score while a host of guardians watch and weep. Our power over human safety seems an unending and fruitless vigil.

Even when protoplasm survives, it still says little about the quality of life. It is here I suffer the worst feelings of unrequited hope. How I wish my charge who has little left in the quantity of his life might yet discover the quality of life.

Has his life any quality? What I must now report will be displeasing. I have suffered a setback. While J. B. was "having a few" at the Mayflower Lounge last night, he met Cassie, a youthful and coquettish human.

Cassie's guardian is an old angel named Alphalite who told me he came from the foundry in Anguria One. He first served the Couriers Elite as the guardian of a Hittite princess before the Lord High Command ever initiated the writing of the book. He knows Featherdraggle and said they roomed together in Upperton at the humanization of Logos. I felt identity in Alphalite's frustration. Cassie is as independent as my client. She, too, pursues her own desires.

It pains me to have to tell you that J. B. brought her to his apartment and . . . the whole episode was most embarrassing to Alphalite and myself with all four of us there together. Not that I haven't suffered through this with J. B. a hundred times before. But I felt he was making such good progress. Nevertheless, nothing could dissuade him. I tried to help him to recall how he felt during the Frankie Williams telecast. His intentions rushed forward toward the act. Even the suggestions of Aunt Ida's broken faith in him would not avail. Had they been man and wife, Alphalite and I would have found the situation a fond and close expression of noble eros. Now we regard the whole affair as but the gluttony of glands—a bogus offering of soul.

What shall I do? The same sentiment my client calls love, the Great Chair labels lust. If J. B. and Cassie could know real love, they would be slow to label their appetites with so grand a word. I grieved to give the night to Daystar, but his will became their burning fever. Reason alone is on God's side. The voltage of human experience is on Daystar's.

The frequent categories of human ecstasy are all his. The planet is crazy about this phenomenon of flesh called so short a word as scarcely makes three letters. SEX, SEX, SEX. It must be said three times to make three syllables. Yet, this silent, screaming inner drive drives men!

The entire planet celebrates its common appetite. They make every possible use of this omnipresent urge. Sex sells soap and autos, hand cream, and clothing. From highway billboards half-naked forms, gargantuan in size, gaze out over eighteen lanes of traffic. These titan nudes smile down in bronze skin to sell the products they espouse. Seductive mouths smile with an intrigue across the void, begging tourists to lust, if only for an instant, as they hurtle down the freeways.

J. B. and Cassie are like their world. It is natural to the both of them to "make love" as they say. They make nothing but tangled psychologies they shall spend the rest of their lives unraveling. What they experience was created in Eden by a lavish Artist, who thought in all His creativity to give the race the gift of intimacy. So to Adam and Eve was given the grand donation—the simple pleasure of skin. It was a tiny ecstasy compared with that great cosmic love the angels know firsthand. But these who never know the best will exalt the least, and this great universal pleasure is their one preoccupation.

What shallow occupations Daystar gives the globe! They follow their passions until the fever in their systems leaves them powerless to control the firestorms of their indulgence. The megavoltage of their eros burns hot till passion electrocutes itself and slumps in weak relief. Then they lie quietly contented in the smoldering aftermath and speak of it as "love" which they are "in" or, indeed, have "made."

Their strange and fiery ritual was over in a furious quarter hour. J. B. had a certain inner knowledge that ecstasy wasn't his by right. But neither of them speak of rightness or wrongness in their relationship. They boast of their liberation from the older, other times. They even then turn on the lights to show how liberated they are. They smoke in bed and speak of their enlightened innocence. They marvel that they feel joy without shame. "We are Aquarian," they said when they had finished. They are strange Aquarians who refresh themselves from foetid jars and call the water clean.

I will not have the Committee think that I believe that their illicit pastime is the greatest of all sins. No, the world bleeds from much greater kinds of moral and social wounds than J. B. and Cassie create. But their own indulgence blinds them to any greater purpose for themselves and dulls the conscience to any definition of grimdeed. They confuse the pursuit of pleasure with the pursuit of happiness.

Oh that they knew what Alphalite and I have dreamed for them! If they could see the Logos swathed in wounds and ready to receive them, they would cry for honest love. They need the wisdom that was His to understand what it really means to be liberated. He cried out during His humanization that man should not call liberty by such lesser names, for self-denial is the only pier upon which real love rests, and commitment is the basis of true love. Love that will not commit itself is too selfish to be love. And that which J. B. calls love allows him to gratify his flesh without making any promises to Cassie. Nor is his love self-denial; rather, it is self-indulgence. They misuse each other and name the usage love.

Human intimacy is not wrong. Indeed, it is the very gift of the High Command to all who dwell upon this planet. But even when it is right, chief of virtues it must not be.

The highest love does not seek sweating starbursts. Neither J. B. nor Cassie can admit this without their self-respect crumbling, though inwardly they know that there must be a higher love that does not get lost in a wilderness of petty appetites. The best love still comes back from hilltops with wounded hands, forgiving all of its assassins.

I remember well the death day of our Logos. The vultures circled the gallows, but He would not leave the world. He hung there just as if He had to do it. He would not abandon those puny nails and come back home. I remember how His heart finally broke, and they laid His body firm against his mother's coarse-cloth dress. She cried. Upperton agreed in anguish.

We had waited for hours with drawn swords, but He would not give the word. I was ready with the rest. We would have made a junkyard of Muddyscuttle, but He forbade it, and we all knew why. Our Logos was in love! IN LOVE with a fallen planet, whose one great reply to His desire was the gallows.

How shall I communicate to J. B. and all such ignorant braggarts who make skin the only definition of love?

> *Call dying love.*
> *Call flesh pretense.*
> *Call human ecstasy a fault.*
> *Call Logos love, all moral sense.*

Alleluia,
Valiant

The Aftermath

J. B.'s liberation is about to destroy him. All his offenses proceed from his inner self. The Logos once said that the human mind is the real culprit in physical gluttony. J. B.'s inner indulgence is constant. His mind enjoys the stream of fantasies that precede every act. He cannot see that his indulgence proceeds from his thoughts. As goes the gray matter, so goes the man. If he would only think higher, he would automatically live more nobly.

Alphalite seems less concerned about Cassie than I do about J. B. Since he was once the guardian of a Hittite princess, Cassie must seem tame to him. Oh, if I were as old and wise as he! I am suffering from a lack of experience, and like most younger guardians, I still have a problem in trying to live on the rarified joy of Muddyscuttle. Isaiah, that unusually gifted Scuttler, once said, "As the heavens are higher than the earth, so are His ways higher than ours." This is a rare insight that I doubt my client will ever discover in the days left to him.

The problem of adjustment might not be so great for guardians if we could remember that our charges represent an entirely different state of being. I must show J. B. that while his physiology is riddled by fierce storms of appetite, nothing eternal exists in the froth and foam.

The word *sex* has the same number of letters as the word *God*. Volumes of symbolism could be based on this correlation. Their urgings may be similar in plane and degree to those fierce and beautiful urgings that I have to praise the Logos. The powerful drive to sing *Gloria in Excelsis* that wells up in my heart is not altogether unlike their short desire to be fulfilled. Without praise I would find existence barren. My fiery lust to serve the Logos sweeps me with a desire to merge in one glorious pinnacle of praise. My being becomes ecstatic. The fire and power of all my urgings is laid at last in joy beneath His feet who makes us soar the cosmos.

This must be how J. B. feels. The task is to teach him that true meaning lies, not in his ecstasy, but in ours. Many Muddyscuttler believers avow this as a spiritual ideal, but find it hard to practice. St. Paul admitted that it was hard for humans to live with celibacy. He permitted sexual intercourse in marriage. Grudgingly he admitted that it was "better to marry than to burn." My charge is following a new, looser rule. He apparently does not like Paul's either/or sexual ethic.

Not all the reclaimed followers of the Logos seek to dispute these urgings with such fervor. I cannot believe the conversion of my client will answer all his appetites with quietude forever. Muddyscuttlers have no end of stories about believers who mismanaged their passions after they came to the Logos. I am always reminded of the truth in such fictions as Elmer Gantry or Hester Prynne. Scarlet Alphas are often given by the church to those who they once believed were chaste. In every generation the church was disappointed that the reputation of her finest servants was sacrificed on so low an altar as a common bed. At least J. B. is not a religious hypocrite covering his sexual escapades with mock piety.

I know that my client's behavior with Cassie is much the product of something that angels never can understand—procreation. We guardians came directly from the foundries of the Spirit. Adam and Eve were the only humans to arrive this directly at being. Since them, Muddyscuttlers have been participating in the process of making people. The hunger that drives human intimacy is part of this divine plan.

For humanity to survive, the High Command had to endow it with the force of sexuality. If I did not know how perfect the Creator is, I might believe He overdid it all.

In the case of my client, I intend to try one new suggestion at the next weekend session he is already planning. I shall get him to keep the lights burning more brightly. As our Beloved once said, "Obedience loves light, while passion feeds on darkness."

> *Whatever was*
> *Was His because*
> *He paid the price*
> *Of sacrifice.*

Alleluia,

Valiant

The Last
of October

The lovers have now spent two weekends together and seem to be settling into a lifestyle.
Their excursions are regular. I was wrong about
Alphalite: he feels that the Hittite princess was
"chaste" compared with Cassie. The princess,
he says, always sacrificed doves to atone for
conscience. Cassie feels no such religious duty.

J. B. and Cassie have a pattern of behavior
that is predictable. After work on Friday they
begin drinking to loosen up. They are usually
quite loose before they leave the lounge. Once
they begin these sessions, it is most difficult to
bring angelic influence to bear. I ever feel sorry
for them. Their naïveté contains a nobility of
spirit, but one that is tightly chained to human
frailty.

Once J. B. brandies his brain, I have trouble
communicating with him. I know now for sure
that it is in his mind that the battle is lost. He
swims in fanciful fornication for an entire afternoon before the actual indulgence in his escapades. I find myself swimming in his muddled
thought amid fantasies and gluttonies of all

sorts. I can only shout idealisms over the roar of the glandular cascade.

If J. B. would take the advice of St. Paul, he might put the voltage of his nervous system to sleep. He could then fill the empty spaces in his conscience with virtue, honor, and nobility. Within a minimum of self-control, he could walk his days with purpose. And he would learn to manage his thoughts, which now manage him.

I am weary these days. My one refreshing thought is that I am spirit and never shall be subject to mortality. Homesickness—that's what it is. It is heightened by the frequent feeling that I am losing the battle with my low-minded charge. I've only a few months to go here and then I shall be home again. How much I would give to know that when I enter Upperton, my charge will be with me. Till then I shall be an angel who stares vacantly into space and sings unheard the distant paean we learned as cherubs:

> Glory be to the High Command
> To His beloved Logos and
> His Agent resident in man.
> Let every guardian angel stand
> And bow his head
> At love like this.

How far away Upperton seems, yet it cannot be. The flesh is so susceptible to injury and death that it never lasts very long. I'll be home before the world's long night begins. Still, I want J. B. with me when I come. This must be! We must come back together! I shall struggle within the confines of his mind and make it happen! I will see to it that his mind is made new! By Upperton, I will!

This is where it all begins and ends . . . the MIND. I know now that Dr. Classie is right. His evangelism is honest. If the mind is straight, the man will be. Everyone is the mirror of his thoughts. Living straight is thinking straight. J. B. heard the sermon—why can't he *do* that sermon?

Conversion is little more than the turning of the mind, and J. B.'s must turn until his mental image becomes his outward form. Murder is not a function of the flesh; it springs from ordinary grudge. Adultery occurs not where skins touch, but where lust is left an unstrangled fantasy. And J. B.'s gray matter prepares the bed of lust for Cassie's pleasure. He considers moral reform, but only after his morality is smudged.

Let us take the glutton. He hates food, but only when his stomach is distended by abundance, which he immediately wishes he could somehow make retroactive. Only when he is stuffed does he desire reform. When he is empty, his mind plays with cream desserts and rich sauces and sweetmeats. Finally in fury he devours all that he had dreamed. He chides himself for his grimdeeds and takes a firm stand that now at last he will reform. Tomorrow only lettuce leaves and water, and all the grimdeeds are paid for.

A Scuttler will take his conscience and train it until it offers him such silent pleasures as he can nowhere else obtain. His imagination will create an image strong enough to last him till he can feed himself with more than images.

I know a guardian to a fundamentalist lecher. The angel is amazed that one can be both a fundamentalist and a lecher. The first time that his client contemplated adultery, the idea was repugnant to him. The second time his mind found some intrigue in the possibility. The third time he permitted his cloistered mind to taste all that it would.

All those who know his Christian life never suspect that he is double-minded. He smiles religiously. He prays with volume that would deafen Heaven. He has split himself into two people, each of whom the other cannot accept. One is a monk and the other is a seething bohemian. The two wear the very same wardrobe yet never meet, so there is never any conflict. It is a safe arrangement by which many Christians manage a double life that appears single in each of its contexts.

I heard of a poor man in France who many years ago was compelled by the state to be an executioner. The first time that his trembling hands raised the bloody blade of the guillotine, he cried, trembled, and wept that he was man. He could not bear to hear the victim screaming and kicking in protesting those who dragged him forward and clamped his straining form in the braces. He closed his ears against the dull thump and turned from the tense neck that lay against gory steel. So it was with the first dozen. Soon, however, he freed himself to look. Then he gazed. At last he rose eagerly on the morning when the executions were scheduled.

The mind will soon permit what it earlier abhorred. I remember the first time that J. B. indulged in illicit sexuality. He was morose for days. Images of Aunt Ida dogged his guilt. He could scarcely eat, he felt so bad. Soon he tolerated his grimdeed. Then he enjoyed it. Now he does not even consider it wrong.

This is the last state of self-acceptance, and the only thing that will cure an easy view of sin is the strong judgment of the Inner Logos. I will not be happy at all until my own unhappy charge has such inner direction.

Perhaps such issues of ethics and philosophy too much enchant me. They may, indeed, paralyze my service unto Him. They have an old proverb on Muddyscuttle: "Fools rush in where angels fear to tread." It is somewhat comforting to know that they at least separate fools and angels. I must be careful that I do not bring the categories closer.

Praise to the birth of things that be.
Alleluia, there was light.
Alleluia, there were seas.
Alleluia, there were beings.
Men immortal, straight as trees.

Alleluia,
Valiant

 # Snow

The first snow of winter has left everything whiter than it was.

I am reeling at the circumstances. It all happened during a long and gentle snowfall. I was aware that something happened when J. B. and I met Alphalite and Cassie at Henry VIII. While this may sound like a museum, it is a bar.

I noticed that Alphalite was in a supreme state of elation. He was buzzing in and out of walls and making frequent Alleluias. It is good that we sing in other dimensions or the bar would have exploded with the sound of his joy.

The fireworks—if the Committee will permit such a terrestrial cliché—began when J. B. offered to buy Cassie a highball and she declined. J. B. had his "usuals," which is no longer unusual, since he is having them unusually often. The excesses of his father more and more mark his life.

Cassie clearly had something on her mind that she knew J. B. would find unpleasant. J. B. insisted that she loosen up with him by having one of her usuals. "J. B.," she said, "I don't want to loosen up. I know what happens every time we get 'loose.'"

J. B. was afraid. "Come on, Cassie, let's unwind—I've got a new kind of chablis I want you to try when we get to my place. It's going to be a great evening!"

"Not for me!" said Cassie.

Cassie was afraid that for her refusal, J. B. would call her a "prude" right on the spot. A prude in Scuttler usage is an over-virtuous woman. But the colloquial malice of the word is a sword upon which the decent soul is skewered. The word is a dreadful curse. American women would rather do anything than be labeled by such a term. There are whole movements of women in this hemisphere that have dedicated themselves to the extinction of such labels.

J. B. looked into his drink, studied the ice cubes, then blurted out, "What are you, Cassie, some kind of prude? For God's sake!"

"Yes, it is rather for His sake, I suppose," she said.

"Whose sake?" thundered J. B., banging his glass of ice cubes on the small table.

"God's."

"God's? Don't tell me you're getting mixed up with God. You're not only a prude, but a God-nut. . . . Cassie, for Christ's sake!"

"His, too!" she said in the face of his hard anger.

A long period of silence followed. It seemed for a moment she might abandon her prudery and agree to go home with him. I have not seen two souls more in agony than they appeared to be. I could tell she wanted to please J. B., but even more than that, she seemed possessed of a new allegiance. He could neither understand nor accept it. She wanted to have a little drink with him, but was afraid that even one might weaken her resolve. He stared at the bottom of his glass.

After an agonizing silence, she spoke nervously, but she was firm.

SP EVELASCO

"Look, J. B., let's face it. We have a cheap relationship, always plastered over with too much booze and a lot of cheap scenes in your apartment."

Alphalite beamed.

"It never bothered you before," he said.

"Well, it does now, since . . ."

"Since what?" he almost shouted. He was talking so loudly that several others in the bar turned their heads and stared in the direction of their table.

"Since what?" he asked again, not quite so loudly.

"Well," she hesitated. The words were coming hard for her.

"Since what . . . Since What . . . SINCE WHAT?"

"Since I accepted Christ."

Alphalite began buzzing excitedly through the walls again.

J. B. blurted out a coarse laugh and slapped his leg in cruel attack. "You accepted Christ! . . . How could you do that?"

I felt sorry that J. B. was so acid to Cassie. The idea of Cassie "accepting Christ" bothered me some, too. The idea is all so humanized somehow. Who are these mortal Scuttlers that they condescend to accept or reject the Logos? The key issue never seems to surface in their small system of arrogance. "Accept Christ" is the way that some Scuttlers in the evangelical world refer to reclamation. I know the Committee will be galled by this, for it seems they may have missed the point. Their way of putting it leaves the Almighty under human judgment. Reclamation is a matter of the Logos condescending to accept man, and not man stooping to accept God. It makes a wreck of excellence.

We dare not dwell long on this kind of human arrogance. Logos-life is offered to them on a silver platter, and they ponder their own ability to accept the magnificent sacrifice. What's for them to accept? They should beg His favor. If they miss it, indeed, all that is left to them is Daystar's Chamber. How fashionable to make their rescue from the pit sound like some sort of bargain for God! What drowning man confers upon the lifeguard a laurel because he has been so lucky as to rescue his resplendent victim?

Since so many speak of it this way, we must not be too hard on Cassie for so phrasing it. In the course of this tense conversation Cassie told J. B. that she had been visited by two "witnesses" from Grace Church who told her about Christ. "Suddenly," she said, "I realized how far I was from the path. I confessed my sin, and I plan to go to church on Sunday. I was hoping you might come too, J. B."

"You're talking like my funny aunt," he replied.

"Ida?" asked Cassie. J. B. nodded. "But you always told me you loved your aunt as anyone else would have loved their mother."

"She's been a mother to me, but she's a God-nut just like you, Cassie," he said in anger again. He seemed suddenly ashamed that he had referred to Aunt Ida with such despicable terms. "Look, Cassie," he said tempering his volume with calm, "if not tonight, couldn't we get together at my apartment this weekend and talk the whole thing over?"

"Not anymore. . . . I'm sorry, J. B. Not this weekend or any weekend. Not tonight or any night! I've come across a new set of standards. I shall need His help to live up to them."

He was offended by the way she spoke of "His help." The divine pronoun *His* is capitalized and often becomes a pronominal substitute for the noun it replaces. It is quite out of fashion on Muddyscuttle to just blurt out the words "Jesus" or "Christ" unless one is using them in a coarse context. The words are used often in bars and lounges, but they are rarely given dignity there. To use the words in the open as you might use the name of William or Eric is taboo. So J. B. was offended at the word *His*. He would have been put off had she spoken directly of Jesus, though she calls our Logos by this familiar name all the time since her conversion.

Soon conversation turned from Cassie's new experience to Grace Church. "What's this place like if it sends out 'witnesses' to menace decent American neighborhoods with God freaks?" asked J. B.

"What's so decent about my neighborhood?" she asked, answering his question with one of her own.

"Well . . . it's . . ."

"I'll tell you what kind of people live in my neighborhood. They drink too much, make free sexuality their lifestyle, and are starved to death for any real piers upon which to build their lives."

"You sound like Frankie Williams."

"Maybe our neighborhoods need to be menaced. Maybe the entire nation could use what I have found. Maybe you need it, J. B. What if your Aunt Ida is right?"

"I still can't fathom people talking about God right in the streets, or in homes, or in lounges like this, for Christ's sake!"

"That's exactly . . ."

"I know, I know, I know—that's exactly whose sake it's for."

"And the people who witness for Christ are not weird. They seem to me to be the only ones in touch with their world. One of the men who shared the Christ-life with me works with your company. His name is Beau Ridley."

"Beau Ridley! I know him. He seemed so intelligent, too. He's the guy who says prayer in the company cafeteria before he eats. . . . I'll be damned!"

"Could be, J. B."

"Cassie, will you quit interrupting me with

84

these innuendos! . . . Beau Ridley," he said collecting himself. "The man's a fanatic! Maybe even a lunatic! So he was one of the—how do you say it?—witnesses who came to your door."

"Yes."

"That phony. How can you let a religious nut like that ruin our great relationship?"

"It wasn't a great relationship. It was cheap! I want out, J. B."

J. B. grew red with anger. "You never were in, Baby!" he yelled at her.

She picked up her coat and purse and walked out into the snow. Alphalite appeared for a moment in the open doorway, and I could see the snow falling.

Alphalite called back in language beyond them, but expressed the wisdom of new creation. "White is a majestic color, Val."

"Indeed!" I called back.

> Power proceeds from purity
> And love grows out of hope.
> Only blackness ever knows
> The shining treasure of the snows.

Alleluia,
Valiant

The Fire
and Image

We are alone tonight. J. B. has had several more of his usuals and isn't thinking very clearly. There is a fire in his fireplace. The room is hot and, yet, there is a chill about it all. He is sweltering from an odd fever set into his system by two loves. One is the attachment he feels to Cassie which I thought was only a sexual convenience. Tonight it is becoming clear that she means more to him than I had before supposed.

The second love is one that he only observed in Cassie. He is almost jealous of her new love for Christ. How can one really be jealous of such an exalted and different kind of love? Yet, he is. Besides this jealousy, he is seething in resentment that Christ has apparently doomed him to lonely weekends.

While he was staring at the fire, the dancing flames seemed to hold him mesmerized. "Why . . . why . . . did she do it . . . I need her so. . . ," he muttered looking again into the fire. "Oh, hell!" he said, throwing his glass against the mantle. It shattered and fell upon the hearth. He barely had spoken the words when the imagery of his words fell upon the flames.

He remembered the fire! It was hell! That fire that so long ago had left him an orphan. He remembered how lonely he felt when he knew his parents were still in their incendiary tomb that had been his tight little world. The teddy bear that had been his only surviving toy still glared at him from its slouch position on the corner of the bureau near the window. "Hell!" he said again.

The fire flickered.

He beheld the image of himself as a boy wandering on the lawn among the great hoses and sirens and red lights. He remembered the fire and his immense gratitude that Aunt Ida had come. How he clung to her in the most welcome embrace of his life! She had been so different from his own parents. Her love, while only a kind of substitute for the new loneliness that was his, had seemed rooted in the firm soil of Kentucky. How he needed that depth of compassion that lived in the good country woman!

Now he wondered if Aunt Ida would even recognize him. He was drunk, lonely, and maudlin over his old rag toy. Nor would International Investors have recognized this budding young executive, oiled in martinis, crying over his teddy bear, and cowering before spectres that rose from his own fireplace to walk his troubled thoughts.

He got himself a drink. With bleary eyes he walked over to the little bear and picked it up. He smiled and felt the pain of bittersweet memories. He set the bear down, and by odd coincidence, its soft left leg fell upon the Bible. He picked up the book. He stood with the amber flickering of the fireplace upon his young yet aging face. "What would Auntie think? My standing here with a Bible in one hand and a martini in the other?" he asked himself.

He thought to read it, but only thumbed through it and set it down again. "Despair for nothing!" he said to himself. "I have all: a fine job, a sports car, a good salary, and an apartment with the right address." Then Cassie's definition of her neighborhood rang again in the air about him: "I'll tell you what kind of people live in my neighborhood. They drink too much, make free sexuality their lifestyle, and are starved to death for any real piers upon which to build their lives." J. B. knew that this was not only her neighborhood, but his as well. Even more than his neighborhood, it was himself.

He looked above the glass. The former one lay shattered on the hearth. The flame reflecting from the broken pieces seemed somehow to symbolize his life.

Then I managed something that I have never tried before with my client. He has somewhat of a strong mind, so I was able to manage this only because he was so drunk as to offer little resistance. A vision formed on the amber tips of the flames that settled low above the glowing coals.

In the dying fire there swam the image of his auntie as she had been years before. Among the smaller embers stood an adolescent image of himself. The smaller grasped the larger. They embraced, and as the boy held her, she grew old and wrinkled, then faded and was gone.

He was alone. He knew he was.

Then there arose a teddy bear. It seemed friendly unto him for just an instant. Then it began to enlarge. Its scruffy little face changed as it grew. Then it loomed above him in the room and towered aloft. It was fanged. His great security symbol now menaced him. It beckoned him into the flames. He was afraid to obey. His fear popped out in perspiration on his forehead. The hypnotic effect of the coals fixed his trance. With effort at last he managed to close his eyes against the demon bear.

He turned himself from the fire and faced the

SEVELASCO

icy windows. "Oh, Auntie, save me!" he said. The cold air near the frosted window brought him a new view of his world. He was ashamed he had cried out into the room. He turned and looked again and the demon was gone. The only bear in the room still stared at him from the bureau top.

"Well, I'll be damned," he said, but wished he hadn't.

> *The things that thump in semi-light*
> *Give substance to all moral fright*
> *And make men fear the pending night*
> *That Heaven never sees.*

Alleluia,

Valiant

Of Love and Backslipping

While J. B. has not seen Cassie since the big snow, I have learned something of her from Ridley's angel, Joymore. She has learned that free love is costly in terms of guilt and self-acceptance. Her former weekends will not set free her present ones. Why did she ever live with J. B.?

Like other Scuttlers, Cassie spends most of her time trying to understand herself. Her psychological probes occupy her, but do not help her. Psychology has existed for a hundred years, but it is still an unsettled science. There are as many theories of human behavior as there are psychiatrists. Cassie has read many in her search for herself. Most psychologists agree that guilt is the enemy of self-acceptance. I have warned Alphalite that he must guard her closely now, for Daystar is working overtime to try to trap her between her new commitment and her old lifestyle.

Evangelical churchmen on the planet talk of a problem that believers call backslipping. Backslipping is the human tendency to abandon the Logos-life and reenter a former value system. It usually begins in self-sufficiency.

✓ The Logos never taught self-reliance. He taught that He Himself is the only source of confident living.

Many Muddyscuttlers use positive thinking as the key to self-control. Unfortunately, positive thinking does not major on the Logos. It is based upon a defective psychology which teaches that humans can do anything they think they can. Isn't this an odd idea? One wonders if all the wars and the horrible inhumanities of every age haven't been based upon such thinking. Alphalite must be sure his client is not misled by such preposterous ideas.

The position is dangerous for Cassie. It inevitably leads new believers to the pit of despair. It all begins and ends in the spirit of human resolve to strive until some quality of life is achieved. "Cast your heart above the bar," said one Scuttler athlete, "and your body will follow your heart." Oh, that Cassie might learn quickly the ugly chasm between intention and human ability!

I have heard that this strange idea of self-reliance begins in youth. Parents on Muddyscuttle allegedly tell their children about a little steam device they call a "choo-choo." There is a childhood tale about a little locomotive who is asked to pull a long line of cars up a hill. The "choo-choo" is a positive thinker who manages to succeed because he believes so much in himself. He goes chortling along the rails saying, "I think I can, I think I can." Humans often read this tale to their children, pointing out that they must become "choo-choos" to succeed. The story is probably a part of Cassie's distant past.

Alphalite told Joymore that Cassie sees herself as omnicapable. Her petty arrogance dismisses most of her need for our Beloved. Her tyranny lies in making God her partner in a faith venture. Like most other positive-thinking Christians, she has two sides: hers and the one which is not so crucial. She has mistakenly felt that the Logos is on her side and is assisting her in a kind of spiritual imperialism to "rise to the top of life." She believes that faith in the Logos gives her the right to control others and be successful, whatever devious path she must follow.

She has already read some of the numerous books and magazines on the subject. She has, therefore, heard a score of Christians testify how God exists on the side of our own personal advancement and career. "How to Be Successful" reads one such article. "Jesus Made Me Corporate Head" reads another. "Christ Gave Me the Winners Cup in Swimsuit Competition" reads another. From what Alphalite tells me, she is still unable to see that her idealism is naïve and motto-ridden. "Turn Your Aches to Steaks" says one; another reads, "Jesus Don't Sponsor No Flops." Here are the simple slogans which, attached to human efforts, shabby as they are, degrade the saving work of the Logos.

My fear is that Cassie may be diverted to areas of her egocentric Christianity which will cause her to be unconcerned about J. B.'s reclamation. That must not happen; her own new faith is the most immediate hope my client has of being reclaimed. Should she backslide at this point, my ardent hope for J. B. would suffer. He is clearly "in love with her" and so smitten by this romantic madness that he would be most open to anything Cassie said. Oh, that she knew this!

Even though I know my time here is short, I must remind the Committee that I am struggling on through storms of homesickness. I have caught myself distracted at cocktail parties as J. B. has his usuals. I feel a certain planetary revulsion in these moments. I find myself singing the silent songs of infinity. How long a human year can seem when one is separated from the Logos! J. B.'s Cassie does not really want to go to Heaven when she dies; better there than the alternative, she feels. But like other Scuttlers, she doesn't want to die at all, so earth, not Heaven, is the residence she most desires.

Here's the nub of such biological spirituality. These evangelicals all sit in dimly lit churches. There they sing of the glory of going to Heaven, but no one wants on the next load. It is hard while you breathe the planet's air to imagine doing without it, even though it is a cumbersome and gummy ether when viewed from our side.

Leaving the planet is a gruesome disinheritance for them. It is because they love too low. Still, they are ardent in their naïve passion. Never would they voluntarily opt for living in a world where flesh is cumbersome; there they cannot glut on all the various pursuits that are their current appetites.

Take ice cream. It is hard for those who crave ice cream to imagine a world without this delicacy. They would rather miss eternity than do without it. And if any among them visualize eternity, they imagine it devoid of ices and sweetmeats, or any other pleasantry.

Scuttlers view Heaven as the next best thing to sex or booze or banqueting or nature walks or sunny beaches. Heaven is just below whatever they happen to enjoy. For such, the Logos is not prize enough to replace the disinheritance that death will bring them.

They are all afraid of death, and this fear is so natural to them that even the love of the Logos does not set them free. With some it is not so much death they fear, but the dying. Dying is not just losing Muddyscuttle, but the hurt that comes in the process of losing it. Only the old apostle makes any sense: "The suffering of this present time is not worthy to be compared with the glory that shall be." This is a difficult thing for people on the planet to believe. A thousand curses on their infernal naïveté.

Oh, how I long for the music that neither J. B.

nor Cassie can even imagine while they are prisoners to protoplasm. Always they will indulge their flesh and starve their spirits.

At my last rehearsal, the Cogdillians were performing the anthem for Clockstop called "Valiant the Rider in Splendor and Power." It is a magnificent piece whose strains will not settle from my spirit. I remember that the bass accompaniment was an exploding supernova and a comet storm. I do so anticipate giving up these shallow orchestrations that Muddyscuttlers call music. It offends all taste. Has the Committee ever heard of a "jukebox"? The deepest part of Daystar's pit must be long arcades filled with the raucous devices.

J. B. still swelters in meaninglessness, precisely because he has no real way of perceiving our parallel universe of spirit. He suffers from nearsightedness, seeing nothing but the obvious, loving only the transient. He sings only jukebox music and, sadly, never suspects the gallant anthems of our realm.

> *Valiant the rider in splendor and power*
> *Comes upon light and the thunder of force.*
> *Eternity bridles the path of the hour*
> *And glory unfolds at the source of the source.*

Alleluia,
Valiant

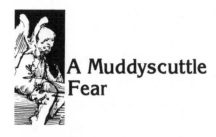

A Muddyscuttle Fear

I have greatly desired to pass along some
spiritual counsel to Alphalite. But I still have
not seen him since that last exchange between
J. B. and Cassie in the bar. It has not been long
in our reckoning of time, but it has been two
weeks for them. I do hope Cassie is still "sticking to her guns," as Scuttlers often say of determined resolve.

One crucial event and several interesting ones
have befallen J. B. First of all, J. B. took a business trip to a city called Los Angeles. I was
hoping it really would be a city of angels, but to
my dismay the same proportion of angels and
guardians exists there as anywhere else on the
planet.

Most interesting was the flight itself. I have
never enjoyed time on an airship. How cumbersome and slow the odd thing went, and yet,
they called it flight. How pedestrian is human
science! We were lumbering along at such a
snail's pace, I wonder that we did not fall upon
the planet. It would not have been a long fall,
but you know how prone these humans are to
injury and death. None would have survived.

Two things happened that caused my client

to think later of the Logos and Cassie's changed values.

The first occurred when the plane made an intermediate stop in a city called Denver. J. B. was approached in the air terminal by a strange group of young people wearing colored robes and chanting strange words I could not recognize. Neither did J. B. They approached him near a newsstand where he had planned to buy a magazine that he refers to as a "girlie book." I will not distract myself to explain "girlie" to the Committee.

He never bought the magazine because these strange young people were trying to sell him a holy book of their own. I reminded J. B. that he had not even read the Holy Bible that his Aunt Ida had given him. I warned him to be careful about buying books of which his Aunt Ida would not approve. The impact of my suggestion was strengthened by J. B.'s reflecting about Cassie and his Aunt Ida and their elusive similarity. He was smitten in conscience and bought neither the holy book nor the girlie magazine.

Later in his hotel room in Los Angeles J. B. made a discovery as he was standing before the mirror shaving. He noticed a large swelling just under his jaw. He stroked it, felt it, and tried to make it retreat into his neck, but he could not. He seemed alarmed by its defiant appearance.

The next morning it was still there. He had a certain uneasiness each time he beheld it in the mirror. It caused him some pain, and he shaved that section of his neck more gently than the rest of his face. However, his concern did not alter his drinking habits. He has been hitting the bottle harder than ever these days.

He seems to have lost interest in the fairer sex. His relationship with Cassie is "on the rocks." By odd coincidence, that is the way he drinks his Scotch—though I feel sure the metaphors are not connected.

He does confuse me with his feelings. He told one of the accountants in his carpool that he thought he might be "carrying a torch" for Cassie. One hopes he will "carry his torch" while she "sticks to her guns." (Aren't these clichés dreadful?) I shall need both his love of her and her commitment to the Logos to draw him on toward reclamation.

We returned from Los Angeles on a non-stop flight. Human aviation would beggar a handicapped angel. They have two good wings on these contraptions, yet they dawdle along at the speed of sound. It was most disconcerting to learn that J. B. could get his usuals even on the airplane. Of course, he did. He never passes them up.

He is still suffering from a general lack of interest in life. He may have a touch of Muddyscuttle depression that is usually called the "blahs"; the state which only serves to make his drinking worse. I am sure now that he is in love. Can you help understand this condition of violent infatuation that these humans experience? I wish J. B. would see Cassie long enough for me to see Alphalite. I would like to find out how she has been behaving. She could possibly be "carrying a torch" as well as "sticking to her guns."

At work yesterday J. B. agreed to have lunch with Beau Ridley, Joymore's charge.

This could be a new breakthrough for the Logos. I am still doing my Alleluias with joy even when J. B. mopes about his apartment with the blahs. Think of me. I should very much like to be at Clockstop rehearsals. I am ever more homesick for Upperton. I shall never forget the joy I felt at the humanization of Logos. Wasn't the place called Bethlehem? It must be far away. They never mention it in Cleveland.

If the Logos comes too soon, my client will surely be lost to Daystar's Chamber. I do hope the Great Chair will delay. It would devastate me never to think of seeing J. B. again. It would not be too bad being on Muddyscuttle when the event occurs. I would for eternity be able to describe the whole event from my planetside view. But I want J. B. with me when it does occur. Thus, I plead time. I assume that Gabriel is still to play the Ankret over all materiality?

There was a cherub I used to play with in the robing room in the upper plaza of Glanry. He is less than an anguria of age. His name is Miltie, and while it is not a very celestial name, he took it, I believe, from a human he much admired who wrote of Paradise and the fall of man in the seventeenth century. Miltie used to look forward to the day when he would take his own place in the Couriers Elite. Before he is old enough to serve, I have a feeling that Muddyscuttle will have undergone Clockstop. It cannot offend him if such be the eternal will of the Logos. Not every cherub can sojourn in materiality; some will be forever in the ideal realm, which daily claims my thoughts.

When any realm gives way,
The universe rejoices.

Alleluia,
Valiant

A Special
Word to
the Committee

My days grow short, my conflicts violent. Here is the essence of my inner wrangling. Humans know only a lateral geography east and west and whatever the other two are. They know nothing about the upper and lower dimensions.

This is most unfortunate because east is about like west, but upper is immensely better than lower, as I am now discovering. The Logos is the example of obedience for both humans and angels. He left Upperton for Muddyscuttle because He loved the Lord High Command who loves every living being in the universe.

I have often marveled at this creation when I can see no reason for its being. I have heard of the planet Hopeton that is similar to Muddyscuttle. It lies yet unspoiled in the starlets of Firehalls Down. It is a lovely stopover where men are as pure as angels, holding the exact same values. What a world it must be! The High Command has grieved since Daystar tricked Muddyscuttle into dying. It requires no effort to love the ideal, so Hopeton, like angels, lives mid-sea in His affection. But here is the tribute to the High Command—He loves this world exactly as He loves Hopeton. Loving unlovely worlds is the best evidence that the High Command exists.

I marvel how the Logos once wept over the lost humans of this planet. At the end of His humanization He grieved their estate even though their behavior was reprehensible. But when He opened His mouth, He only begged the Great Chair to forgive the planet.

All Upperton fell and wept.

Now I am learning how much the fallen planet means to the High Command. I think I care too much for J. B. I am beginning to know the terrible pain of Logos' love. Oh, that Muddyscuttle might receive it before the air about her insolent existence comes ablaze with justice!

For the sake of J. B. I would like to see the Termination Event delayed. Still, I am eager to sing in the Clockstop Chorus. But time is the enemy here. Scuttlers are always battling the clocks! Even those who live to be old are soon out of time.

I do maintain a secret hope for J. B.'s Aunt Ida. According to a friend of mine in Human Petitions, she is regular in her prayers and many of her petitions focus on her dear nephew. She is concerned for "his soul," as she phrases it. So there are at least two of us down here who care. Perhaps Cassie is praying for J. B., too, but I cannot be sure, since I have not seen her or Alphalite in weeks.

The lump on J. B.'s neck may have little relevance, but it is getting larger, and he is frightened. My clients on earlier tours also became concerned about the various lumps and bumps that came upon them. I do remember that some of the bumps were called "mumps." (You would think they would have called them bumps.) While they caused my charges a great deal of discomfort, I couldn't help thinking about how humorous they were, these

"mumps." Oh, the great day when both J. B. and I will be free of mumps and bumps and time! Isn't it odd that mumps and time both resulted from the planet's revolt?

Mumps seem not to be so terminal a state as being "in love." It has such a profound effect on my client. He is lost these days, rubbing his poor neck and grieving Cassie's absence. He can barely stand to eat. Whether you the Committee can accept it or not, he is "in love." And shallow as it may be to Heaven, it is a deep matter in Cleveland.

> *In little worlds*
> *Is little love.*
> *Small men and tiny worlds should know*
> *Great love will make a planet grow.*

Alleluia,
Valiant

January

Here is the astounding news! J. B. went to a physician, who told him he must enter a hospital as soon as possible. The lump on his neck is of immediate concern. The doctor said it is an unusual swelling that might be an indication of lymphatic carcinoma. This is a serious human condition and far more to be feared than mumps. J. B. is to have a biopsy immediately.

He was so alarmed that he quickly called Aunt Ida and asked her to pray. Aunt Ida plans to come to Cleveland straightway. The biopsy may be immediately preliminary to more serious surgery.

J. B. is so frightened, he is trying to read the Bible again. He threw away most of his girlie books, keeping only the best, which are really the worst. He has been trying to live in a way he feels will please his Aunt Ida. This is a secondary reason for being good, at least when it is compared with the high motives of the saints. But while he is being good for the wrong reasons, he is managing an unbelievable amount of reform. He is to go into the hospital next Monday.

Here is the spectacular news! He is going to

church with Beau Ridley on Sunday. I think there are two reasons: First, he knows that Cassie attends Grace Church, and he is anxious to catch a glimpse of her. Second, he is frightened by the prospect of surgery. He hopes to arrange a last-minute impression on the Lord High Command. He would like to get "God on his side," as he said in accepting Beau's invitation.

He and Beau had an interesting conversation over dinner. I must try to tell you exactly what transpired. They ordered a rather expensive human food called lobster tails. I wish I could draw you a picture of these delicacies as they lay on the plate. When I saw these tails, I wondered what their heads must have looked like.

After the food was served, Beau asked if he could say grace.

"Grace? Right here in the restaurant?" asked J. B.

"Yes . . . if that's all right?" asked Beau.

"Why yes, I . . . I guess so."

Beau did pray rather loudly, and J. B. looked around at other guests and smiled nervously. Mercifully for J. B., Beau's prayer was short.

"I used to pray when I was a boy," said J. B. sheepishly.

"Oh, really. . . . Do you now?" Beau responded.

"Not so much. . . . In fact, I leave that to my Aunt Ida. She's more regular than a preacher."

"What did you pray when you were a boy?"

"Oh, you know . . .

"Now I lay me down to sleep,
I pray the Lord my soul to keep.
If I should die . . ."

At this point J. B. stopped and felt the lump. He seemed choked for a moment and then continued,

". . . before I wake,
I pray the Lord my soul to take."

Taking a bite of his lobster tail, Beau asked, "And if you did, would He?"

"If I did *what* would He do *what*?" J. B. responded, making it clear Beau's question was confusing.

"If you should die before you wake . . . would He take your soul?" asked Beau.

"I . . . I . . . I guess so. I mean, my Aunt Ida is a special friend of His and . . . I . . ."

"I'm sure she is, but Christ will not accept you on the basis of family faith. Your Aunt Ida's faith cannot avail for you. J. B., you need a relationship of your own with Christ, just like your friend Cassie has."

By this time J. B. was ill at ease. He clawed at his collar, then seized on Cassie's name. "Have you seen Cassie lately?" asked J. B., growing tense.

"Yes. She has become regular at church. I frequently see her in worship. Cassie seems to have made a sincere commitment to Christ . . . but she seems a little lonely. . . . My wife seems to think she's in love . . ."

"With whom? How can your wife tell?" J. B. seemed to be on the edge of apoplexy.

"She may be entirely wrong," said Beau. "Women seem to understand such things. I'm quite pleased with her determination to serve Christ. She really seems to be 'sticking to her guns.' You know, I think my wife might be right. She does seem a little misty-eyed and faraway. I think she may be 'carrying a torch' for someone."

I was delighted with Ridley's insight: So, she is "carrying a torch" and "sticking to her guns" after all. It was welcome news.

The conversation resulted in J. B.'s promising to attend Grace Church Sunday morning. In the afternoon he'll be going to the hospital shortly after Aunt Ida arrives in Cleveland, so his Sunday will be busy.

There is one more aspect of glory. Frankie

Williams is coming to Municipal Stadium with his Greater Cleveland Conquest. Beau mentioned it to J. B. He said he would be counseling inquirers on the field each evening.

Maybe all these circumstances will leave my client open to a new consideration of the Logos. J. B. seems to be more spiritually sensitive in every area. I don't mean to bore the Committee with trivia, but J. B. actually tipped his hat to a nun. A nun, you may recall, is a feminine celibate from the Catholic sororities. Perhaps it is not a great sign in itself, except that in his heart J. B. was thinking, "I must see what these creatures believe that gives them the ability to live without sex." He is obviously still struggling with the involuntary celibacy that Cassie's reclamation has imposed upon him.

One more brief evidence of his progress toward light, and I close. Cars, those curious five-seater vehicles that humans drive, have bumpers. These are *a priori, a posteriori* shock absorbers to cushion accidental impacts. Humans often paste little slogans on these bumpers so that other motorists may read them as they hurtle along at the snail's pace of fifty miles per hour. (This is even slower than their airplanes fly.) These bumper proverbs are curious. Some of these adhesives bear "Christian" messages such as IF YOUR GOD IS DEAD, TRY OURS. While I do not understand them all, a very popular one reads, HONK IF YOU LOVE JESUS. J. B. actually honked and waved the other morning. While there is some possibility that you can honk and not love Jesus, I have this feeling that he is serious in his heart.

I am hopeful that with the lump, Aunt Ida, Frankie Williams, Beau Ridley, Grace Church, and above all, Cassie, maybe J. B. will soon discover the Logos. I would count it all joy if we could set the Couriers Elite to rejoicing over J. B.'s reclamation.

Ah, if it happens! Greatness will come! J. B.

will see a world where he can be of service. He will hear the cry of orphans for the first time. He will see the dispossessed and homeless. He will read beyond his questionable magazines the literature of a suffering world. He will be born anew to the possibilities of a life that is courageous enough to look upon all the hurt that exists just beyond the blind indulgence of all his cravings.

Come, Logos!

> *A star exploded and*
> *The fiery band*
> *Held at its heart*
> *The Great Command to LOVE!*

Alleluia,

Valiant

Star
Thoughts

Things seem to be coming my way at last. I must strike while the iron is hot, as they say in my arena. My fear is that I may be pinning too many of my hopes upon the coming Frankie Williams Conquest.

The danger of conquests is that they are often emotional in their appeal. Reclamation at its basic level is the sovereignty of the Logos. Only last week I learned that several were turned back at the gates of Upperton. They had terminated in a car crash on the way home from some evangelistic worship services. They had arrived at the gates singing sweetly a song they had heard at the conquest. It was with some terror that they were turned back, for they had no real knowledge of the Logos.

I am always sad for those who have a form of religion but fail to understand real faith. No one is admitted to Upperton except those filled with the substance of the Logos. I cannot allow my client to rely on shallow understanding. The world swelters under a thousand griefs: death, war, hate. He must be reclaimed or he will never care about the things Upperton cares about.

During the time our great Logos was a common Scuttler, He observed much shallowness of spirit. He warned all Scuttlers, "Not everyone who cries Logos shall enter Upperton, but he who does the will of the High Command." It is the will of the High Command for men to fill their hollow existence with service to a broken world.

My client must constantly face this issue of inwardness. Upperton is off-limits to Scuttlers whose only attribute is outwardness. I remember a surprised atheist who came to the gates unable to believe he was still alive when he knew he wasn't. He was trying to get in without the inwardness that is the one inviolable standard of Upperton. He was honest, having come straight from the philosophy department of a large university. He kept mumbling that he had many degrees and had never seriously believed in either Upperton or the High Command. He assured us that finally he knew that both were as real as the Philosophy Department. But he was so late in coming to us that, of course, we could do nothing to help.

I fear that J. B. may be frightened into shallow commitment by this lump. He may make some spurious decision because of his love for Cassie. Nevertheless, he must receive the Logos out of his own sense of spiritual desperation or he, too, will be turned from the gates.

Most Scuttlers have fuzzy notions about what it takes to be admitted. I once knew a man who arrived at the office of Credentials Assessment offering his God-and-Nationhood badge earned in Young Campers. He insisted it wasn't fair to turn him down when he had helped so many old ladies across the street. I would have helped if I could, but his name was missing from the Logos' Journal, so I was powerless.

J. B. must come to understand that the nature of reclamation lies in the Logos' demand that true penance be offered in the stead of human arrogance, or inwardness has no validity.

Scuttlers always codify and reduce the mysteries of their spirituality to clichés. (This grievous tendency is behind the "Honk-If-You-Love-Jesus" syndrome which I mentioned.) One American evangelist from the Bible Belt codified the mystery of reclamation to a most curious procedure. He called it the "Thessalonian Turnpike to Salvation." There were three lanes on the Thessalonian Turnpike, he said: Lane One, all must turn from sin to be saved; Lane Two, all should follow Jesus to be saved; Lane Three, we must turn to the living God to find salvation. His approach, little different from one of J. B.'s sales seminars, is: Ring the doorbell, while angels presumably come to attention, and say, "Excuse me, sir, but if Jesus were to come this minute, would you be holding a harp or a pitchfork?" If the answer is "harp," well; but if "pitchfork," then you should begin the presentation of the "Thessalonian Turnpike to Salvation."

But even worse than this codification is the "push-pull" approach to the whole subject of penance. Collegians for God has popularized the concept of penance in a booklet called "How to Be Truly Sorry for Sin in Three Easy Steps." The subtitle is "Even Beginners Can Accomplish True Sorrow in Only a Few Moments a Day."

My fear is that J. B. could be led down a path of Christianity where the machinery is great and the mystery small. Although I will rejoice at any experience which brings him to the Logos, he must know that salvation is in the Logos alone and not the rote schemes that evangelicals use to pry apart the gates of heaven. It is never in the best interest of Upperton or Muddyscuttle when the Great Chair is obscured by petty formulas.

Once more my hope rides on circumstance. I

must trust in the combined influences of Aunt Ida, the neck lump, Frankie Williams, Grace Church, and Beau Ridley.

> *Alleluia to the Name of Light,*
> *Alleluia to the place*
> *Where the wounded hand of joy*
> *Beckons littleness to Grace!*

Alleluia,

Valiant

The Rural Saint

I am in church trying to focus on the sermon. The pastor has ability at communication. The circumstances all are blessed. The sermon is on life after death. Nothing could be better for J. B. His neck being what it is, he is most concerned about his future and all the information he can get on Heaven, as the pastor even now refers to our beloved Upperton.

The sermon is obviously being preached by a man who has never been there. Yet those around me this morning are listening intently as though he has just come back from the place. Fortunately they are unable to see the pastor's guardian, who is standing beside him grimacing at his naïveté. It is difficult for these pedestrians to speak of Glory. How shall humans ever learn what angels find so commonplace?

I remember well the time back in Cogdill when I tried to explain to Miltie the Glorifex Factor. It is such a mature idea that I hesitated to bring it up. But he was attentive and seemed to have no trouble absorbing the concept. He would have been a natural for the new star foundries or asteroid outposts, since he has so little trouble with good angelic science. In one

sitting he learned the background of the formula:

The Lord High Command
In Glory Expands.

Miltie's mind quickly grasped that Glorifex is
equal to Magnificence times Expansion, divided by the cube of New Space. How eagerly
he learned the thrilling concept which states
that while the universe is in constant expansion, the magnificence of High Command is
expanding at the same rate, so that no part of
space is ever void of His presence. These poor
Scuttlers listening now to this sermon cannot
even manage the science of a cherub, yet they
do listen intently—especially J. B.

I remember how excited I was when I first
learned of the expanding preeminence of the
Lord High Command. Miltie was dumfounded
to learn that, not only does the great light
spread, but it becomes ever more intense in
those areas where it has always existed.

Perhaps the Committee can tell by my last
letter that, while my enthusiasm is better, I am
still suffering from the dingy illumination of
Muddyscuttle. At least this sermon makes me
see again the delightful world that is only a few
months away now. I anticipate the glorious day
I shall return to Upperton; I shall blink for days
in the incandescence.

I am glad J. B. is hearing of the other world
this morning. How he needs to learn of it! He
will never be drawn very far by tipping his hat
to female clerics. I must say, it is deflating to
leave my own celestial occupations and deal
with nuns and bumper stickers. But I shall seek
to keep our friendship usable across the reaches
of our worlds. And sermons like this one bring
our worlds closer. J. B. doesn't know it, but
only as he accepts my world will his really have
any meaning.

I have continued to meditate upon the words of the pastor. Perhaps that is the mark of a great sermon. It was clear even as he spoke that he had never been to Upperton, and yet there was a fundamental worth to all he said. It was he himself that impressed me. What the man was preceded all he said; isn't it always that way?

He was in league with the angels. He was standing firmly on the planet but free of materiality. He spoke about the reality of the Logos and cried in an honest passion I have not seen to date on this orb. Mystery clung about him, and yet, he was stripped to a nudity of soul and power of essence. He seemed to give full human vision to those things which do not appear. His manhood was there, but only the slightest encumbrance to his inwardness. His words, gilded with joy, flew at J. B.'s encrusted resistance.

J. B. had attended these services to see Cassie. She sat a half-congregation away from him, but once the sermon began, he never saw her again. He did see his sodden interior and thin veneer of respectability. He was close to reclamation as the sermon ended—I am sure of it.

After the service Cassie greeted him with reservation, but welcomed him to the services of *her* church. (Evangelicals tend to be possessive of churches. They know the church belongs to the Logos, but you rarely hear them say so.) J. B. *is* in love. He was dying for her to say something, anything, to him. She maintained her reserve. He asked if he might call her sometime, but she said that there was too much between them. She told him she needed to put some distance between her past and herself. "I would prefer that you not call," she said kindly but firmly.

She turned to walk away when he said, "Very well, Cassie . . . if you could remember to say a little prayer for me, I'd appreciate it. I am going into the hospital today. My doctor is concerned

that I may have a malignancy. I'm distressed
. . . frightened, I guess."

Cassie turned back and tried to speak. She
choked. She tried a second time, but was still
overcome with emotion. Finally, saying nothing, she turned and walked away. Her steps
were weighted with an agony of soul that made
it clear even to J. B. that she was in love. In
spite of the agony of this abruptness, he was
ecstatic to see her so visibly affected.

Alphalite told me in a brief exchange that
Cassie has been picking at her food and is very
much in love. He says she is determined never
to tell J. B. because of her love for the Logos.
She still feels a lot of guilt over her past relationship with my client. She will not leave her past
where she lived it. She presumes against our
Logos by not letting Him forgive the kind of life
that she and J. B. once shared.

Cassie's friends at Grace Church have coun-
seled her to forgive herself all that has already
been forgiven by the Logos. She should live in
the freedom of reclamation. Still she suffers. To
be guilty of guilt is the greatest affront to God.
Guilt is man's great reprimand. Scuttlers are so
reluctant to let the Logos provide atonement;
there is ever the feeling that they must pay for
their own grimdeeds. As if they could! Why
can't they accept the abusive crucifixion they
forced upon our Beloved? What is this foolish
notion that they can pay for their grimdeeds
just by feeling bad about them after they have
been fully forgiven in Heaven? How dare they
think their little acts of self-incrimination are
even visible beside the grandeur of His sacrifice. Yet that's what guilt is: The foolish attempt to purchase forgiveness with their own
moral poverty. Cassie must gain the wisdom to
lay her guilt aside and move from her gray salvation into the full light of moral freedom.

J. B. ate a lonely lunch after the services. He
drove to the airport to pick up Aunt Ida, who

arrived on one of those dawdling airships I mentioned earlier. She got off the plane with a small valise and a large Bible. J. B. was most happy to see her! I spent a few moments getting reacquainted with Nova, Ida's angel; he's a regular sort, solidly attendant. Nova says that, while Ida has certain idiosyncrasies I might find tedious, she practices utter submission to the Logos.

After the initial hug and kisses, J. B. and Ida passed some idle chatter. He said he had been living just "like she had taught him." He was uncomfortable with his own words. She promised to make him kolaches and liver dumplings just as soon as he was out of the hospital. (Aunt Ida was once married to a Slavic man who ate unusual food.) This promise did not seem an incentive to health to me, but it did to him. I suppose it was not too unusual for someone who eats the tails of lobsters.

After visiting for an hour or so about old acquaintances and their welfare, Ida drove J. B. to the hospital. He checked in and went to his room. As soon as he was dressed in the curious bedclothes, Aunt Ida came in and visited until his supper was served. At one point the dialogue became interesting. Nova and I made some rough notes on what they were saying, and here is how it went:

Aunt Ida asked him with great concern, "Jay-Jay, are you worried about your surgery?"

J. B. answered with more than a little anxiety, "What will I do, Auntie, if it is cancer?"

"Do you remember what I taught you when Uncle Harvey was alive?"

"You taught me so many things, Auntie, I can't think of which one you mean right now."

Aunt Ida became forceful. She leaned on the hospital bed and moved in close and said, "Jay-Jay, I mean what I taught you about Jesus bein' the answer to your every problem. Are you still talkin' to Jesus, Jay-Jay?"

J. B. was clearly nervous. "Some, Auntie."

"Some. SOME! What are you saying!" Ida's voice rose higher. "I find that when people only say they are talkin' *some* to Jesus, they really aren't saying anything."

J. B. decided he would be honest. "Oh, Auntie, I can't lie to you. I don't talk to God. I didn't even think there was a God until recently . . . now, I don't know. Maybe there is and maybe there isn't."

"Jay-Jay! What do you mean, you don't know if there is a God?" She became animated and waggled her index finger just under his nose. "Why, if Uncle Harvey—God rest his soul— could hear you talkin' this way, he'd turn you 'cross his overalls and give you what-for. He'd beat these funny notions out of your head for sure."

"I don't know if you can beat atheism out of people or pound God into them," he said.

"Maybe not, but it just isn't right for you to be here, created by the Good Lord and say the Good Lord didn't make you. 'Member them little brown coveralls I made you in the third grade?"

"Hmmm, hmmm."

"Well, the coveralls had a maker, didn't they? And no matter how much you or anybody else would say they didn't, they did." Ida's home-spun logic seemed to J. B. like something he once dredged from a philosophy course—only more rustic.

"I know that, Auntie."

"Well, you're a lot more certain about the coveralls than you are yourself, Jay-Jay. You think you just sorta sauntered into being without any God at all?"

"I dunno. Maybe."

"Maybe! Is that what your professors taught you down at that fancy school? When I think of all the money Uncle Harvey and I spent educating you, too. Did they teach you that there is no God? Did they teach you that He didn't make you whole and perfect?"

At this point she seemed to be through making her point. Then she gathered herself and began again without giving J. B. a chance to reply.

"Well, let me tell you, Jay-Jay, God made everything, and He made it whole and perfect. He never made anything that wasn't perfect and fine . . . except, maybe professors."

"And carcinoma, maybe. Did God make that, too, Auntie?"

"Aha! So that's it, isn't it, Jay-Jay! You are not so much doubting God as you are just plain mad at Him! Well, why didn't you say that in the first place? Everybody gets mad at God every once in a while—even your Uncle Harvey!"

"Well, what's He ever done for me?" J. B. asked, waiting for Aunt Ida's wisdom to deposit security on the threshold of his mind.

"What's He ever done for you?—I'll tell you what! He gave you an aunt and uncle to care for you after your folks were killed in the fire. And He gave you a good mind and a college education. He gave you a good job. He gives you fifteen breaths a minute and a pulse of sixty-eight. He gave you—"

"Carcinoma!"

"No! A THOUSAND TIMES NO! He doesn't do things like that, Jay-Jay! But after everything else He's done for you . . . how can you turn thumbs down on God? One little neck lump and you are all through with Him, is that it?"

"Lately, Auntie, you'll have to admit, God's been walking by me and kicking me every chance He gets. I've got a better-than-average chance of cancer, and I've lost Cassie—"

"Cassie? Who's she?"

"Oh, nobody . . . just a girl I lived with . . . I mean . . . dated for a while, that's all."

"How'd you lose her?" asked Ida, probing

uncomfortably as I cheered and winked at Nova.

"Well, she got religion and won't have anything to do with me anymore."

"Why not? What've you been up to that turns off decent folks?" Ida still probed.

"Er, nothin', Auntie. I'm decent . . . it's just that . . ."

"Now, Jay-Jay, you gonna hold out on Auntie? What have you been doin' that isn't proper? You haven't been philandering 'round here in Cleveland, have you?"

"I don't want to talk about it anymore, Auntie. I have to be up early in the morning for the biopsy."

J. B. was perspiring by this time as Aunt Ida was clearly closing in. As she drew the strings of her pursuit, he became anxious. She opened her big black Bible and read him the most ominous words: "The fool hath said in his heart there is no God." Then she closed the book and took his hand and prayed with sincerity and great volume. She sounded like a prophetess in a thunderstorm:

> Now, God, Jay-Jay doesn't know any better than to say You don't exist. So You gotta help him, 'cause he's scared to death. God, if You wanna heal that little old lump on the side of his neck, You just take it away. I'm gonna have to ask You for this and trust You for it, cause poor Jay-Jay's in no shape to ask You for anything . . .

Her tone became earnest, and tears began to flow from her tightly closed eyes. She continued:

> Oh, God, my poor Jay-Jay's been so lost in his sin and now Cassie's turned her back on him and his low ways. I pray You'll help him be more what he needs to be, not jus' so Cassie can respect him, but so he can respect himself. Mostly, God, give some direct attention to that little lump o' cancer under his jaw. I'm just trusting him to You and Jesus. Amen.

121

When Aunt Ida finished, she kissed him on the forehead. Shortly she gathered up her Bible and her handbag and left the hospital room. She had a less scholarly but a deeper impact upon him than the pastor at Grace Church. He was glad to be alone and yet he wasn't. Nova and I could hardly take notes on their conversation for cheering Aunt Ida. She was magnificent! I hope we can get her into Upperton without revision.

Now the hospital is quiet. J. B. is not quite asleep. He's wishing that he had stayed after worship this morning to talk to the pastor. He is neurotic on most issues of the spirit. One moment he is an atheist and the next a desperate seeker. Still, in his seeking moments, he will not yield to the Logos. He does seem to feel the burden of his previous life with Cassie; at such moments he feels he has sinned against the High Command. The next moment . . . there is no High Command. Human nature is fickle beyond description.

I am on the side of Nova's client. How can any Scuttler stand in the middle of our universe and judge the Great Chair to be nothing at all? Human arrogance reaches its apex in atheism. I found myself wishing that Aunt Ida could become a mandatory lecturer to every university philosophy department. Her wisdom is uncongested. How well she understands the intellectual tendencies of men! They force the Lord High Command into nothingness and by this devious process rise to the spot He had occupied. They are to be pitied.

Aunt Ida has a formulated faith, to be sure. Her view of grimdeeds is as small as J. B.'s, for different reasons. J. B. has been blinded to the great injustices of this world by his own hedonistic ego. Ida's view of grimdeeds has been rehearsed in the puritan atmosphere of American fundamentalism, where drinking and sex are the great grimdeeds denounced often while the universe aches of genocide and economic oppression.

But she is alive to the hurt that afflicts her world. She cares, and she has demonstrated a quality of compassion that can come only from the Logos and the whole substance of inwardness which He imparts.

Tomorrow my client shall know whether his life is to be shortened by disease. It is a heavy night for me. I love him and wish he didn't have to suffer. But from moments like these, our Beloved often gains substance in the human heart.

> *Come lift our Beloved where nothingness lies*
> *And see Him leave footprints in air,*
> *Congealing the vacuum of empty black skies*
> *And reigning where flesh may not dare.*

Alleluia,

Valiant

The End
of Winter

I am learning the dilemma of men. Martin of Wittenberg, who came to Upperton only a few centuries ago, said that man is *simul iustus et peccator*—at once saint and sinner. Here is a cliché that fits humanity in general and my client in particular: "He is mixed up." I should think there is little "up" about being "mixed." I should rather have it "mixed down," since there is nothing elevated or lofty in the kind of indecision that J. B. now deals with. Thankfully, *we* cannot be "mixed up," since Upperton enjoys the complete integration of every value.

J. B. may be deliberately choosing indecision because it is a safer way. Procrastination always eliminates the immediate risk. "The safest of all courses is to doubt," one old Scuttler said. In the battle for any truth we may be vanquished. Doubt only peeps cautiously over the ramparts to watch the battles of those who have the courage to state their convictions.

I cannot force J. B. out of his mixed condition. Uncertainty about values results in confusion. My client is always asking about the value of Logos-life while he clings to the value of life as it is. He conceives reclamation to be the restrictions of the Lord High Command who enjoys breathing down the collar of his loose morality. He has accepted the axiom of his peers: "God is a kill-joy." Part of J. B. wishes to be under a higher dominion. On the other hand, his ego rebels fiercely in favor of his spurious independence from all outside spiritual intervention. The reclaimed often talk glowingly about the "Lordship of Christ" while they live in the conflict of their own lordship. Here is their neurosis: Shall they have a Lord or be a lord? It keeps many from reclamation, and it keeps most of the reclaimed from a better joy. Few resolve it.

Scuttlers have a burden that we Couriers never deal with—flesh! I know I have earlier in this report lamented its absence at moments when I would like to give my client a reassuring touch. But for all the good qualities of flesh, I have never been able to understand the control this infernal substance has over spirit. What is it? Protoplasm? Bones? Follicles? Sinews? Whatever it is collectively, it makes demands. It drives earthlings until they become gluttonous in their appetites and overfill every desire. And ultimately flesh destroys life, for it gets worn and old and diseased.

J. B. is sick—his flesh betrays his well-being. He suffers the curse of the neck lump! There is a real chance he could die from this betrayal of his flesh. He cannot imagine getting on without this 180 pounds of substance he believes to be himself. So he lacerates himself with the possibility of disease. Oh, that he could see the liberation of spirit! It would end his captivity!

> There comes but one great liberty
> When morning wakes the world afresh
> And men shed old, stale bonds to see
> The thaw unfreeze their solid flesh.

Alleluia,
Valiant

The Middle
of the Year

During the night J. B.'s neck lump deflated
and disappeared. The surgeon made a "preliminary incision" but found nothing. J. B. had
extensive testing here at Memorial Hospital,
but nothing has confirmed the early fears. It
appears J. B. has been "healed," as churchmen
say.

He is ecstatic! He is giving credit to Aunt Ida
and God—in that order, I'm afraid. Aunt Ida
has now asked the Lord to give him spiritual
health as well. I owe the order and correctness
of these notes to Nova.

When J. B. emerged from surgery groggy
with anesthetic, he said with murky cheer, "Hi,
Aunt Ida."

"'Ello, Jay-Jay," replied his aunt. "Did you
see the Lord in any of those dreams?"

"No, I didn't see anybody," he said. Then
coming to himself, he quickly asked, "Is my
surgery over?"

"It's all over. And best of all, there isn't anything under that big bandage on your neck."

"What's that?" he responded as though he
had not heard her properly.

"It's all over. There isn't any neck lump.

There wasn't when you went into surgery. The doctor said he'd never had a case like this. The tumor just seemed to go away in the night."

"What are you saying, Auntie? They didn't take the tumor off my neck?" His question represented his incredulity.

"They didn't need to, Jay-Jay. There wasn't any tumor there."

"That's amazing!"

"The word is miraculous! Your doctor said he thought it was amazing, too. But I asked him what was so amazing about the Lord healing my little Jay-Jay."

"Auntie, you're a marvel!" he said as if he had just faced the Virgin of Lourdes.

"Jesus is the marvel!" said Aunt Ida, giving the credit where it was due. "I'm just glad to be His child and able to see Him work His marvelous power in every life—especially yours, Jay-Jay. I'm gonna pray right now and thank Jesus for beatin' these fancy doctors to that neck lump." So saying, she clamped her eyelids together and began.

> Now Jesus, You took care of Jay-Jay and healed him completely. I'm just gonna pray now that You'll help him quit saying You don't exist. He doesn't really mean anything, Lord. You know he's always been a questioning child and he thinks he's being honest with himself. At least now he knows that You can deal with cancer, and he needs to see You heal his doubts and confusion, too. Lord, about his low life; You've seen ever'thing he's done—and I'm sure he's had the angels blushing 'round the throne. Lord, I pray You'll help him give up all his sin and act like Uncle Harvey and I raised him. And Lord, help Cassie—whoever she is—not to be too highbrow and goodie-goodie to help Jay-Jay till he comes around. Thank You for every little blessing from Your mighty hand. In Jesus' name, Amen.

Much transpired in the past twenty-four hours. Aunt Ida left yesterday, but I wish she was still here. There is a kind of power in her rural faith one does not often see around the city.

One other incident you should know about. Cassie brought Jay-Jay . . . rather, J. B. . . . a box of nougats. It was good to see Alphalite again.

Cassie was delighted to learn of the "miracle." She said, "God, indeed, was merciful." J. B. was excited that she had come to see him—was surprised and delighted. She could not stay long. J. B. asked if he could phone her when he left the hospital. She said it would be okay, but she was becoming more involved in church activities and was often not home in the evenings. She said that she was going with the gang to a "Christian Life Seminar" and would be involved for several weeks. When the seminar was over, she agreed that he might call. J. B. asked her for a "good-by kiss." She declined. She said they both had their lives to live, and little good could come of opening old wounds.

As she spoke of "wounds," she glanced at the bandage on J. B.'s neck, then quickly looked away. She walked briskly out of the room. She is determined not to be in love with him, though her determination seems to be weakening.

Beau Ridley called. Because of the miracle, he was able to secure two promises. First, J. B. promised to go to Grace Church again on Sunday. Second, he agreed to attend the Williams Conquest of Greater Cleveland when it begins next month.

In spite of the miracle, J. B. was glum the rest of the evening. I find myself participating ever so slightly in his mood. I understand Cassie's effort to break with her old way of life, but I almost wish she wouldn't be such a "prude."

J. B.'s miracle, which seemed so glorious in the morning, was an uninteresting event by evening. I cannot understand how the glory of his miracle has so soon faded and does not mark his experience more deeply.

There seems nothing more of importance to report. I still seek J. B.'s reclamation. But on the day of a great miracle, I am less hopeful than I should have supposed.

Immediately after his recovery J. B. fastened a great deal of theological importance to the miracle. And for his sake, it may be well. Still, contemporary miracles are less basic to the nature of faith than generally supposed. Miracles do little real good in helping people come to faith or in confirming them in it. They need, rather, that process of inwardness which feeds daily on spiritual substance. Only then will they adore the Logos more than His acts.

J. B.'s miracle meant more to him in the morning than it did in the evening. And yet, to quote the Book from another context, "The evening and morning were the same day." How quickly the light fades.

Oh, that he might know the Scriptures. Scuttlers suppose that if they could only see something "un" or "super" natural, they would immediately come to faith. Now J. B. has arrived at point-blank truth. God has affirmed Himself in personal power at the point of J. B.'s great physiological need. He has seen the magnificent evidence of the supernatural. Yet he doubts. The miracle meant more to Aunt Ida than to J. B. She didn't need the miracle to believe in God; she believed in God as much before it happened. J. B. still disbelieves in spite of it.

Faith neither begins nor grows by miracles. The Logos chose the route of humanization in the glorious process of Muddyscuttle's reclamation. But this miraculous experience has never been witnessed by Muddyscuttlers as a whole. "Eye knowledge" is important to Scuttlers. They have a proverb here that says "Seeing is believing." What a curious dependency! The corollary proverb is damning: "Not seeing is doubting."

Isn't it odd that having seen the supernatural, J. B. has regarded it so naturally? Why won't he learn that believing comes first and seeing later? If he would believe, he would see all that now mystifies and perplexes him. He would join the liberated Scuttlers for whom miracles are evidence to the heart and not the eye.

My client would be reclaimed already if he could accept his own spirituality. His thinking is materialistic. If he were pulverized to fine ash and scattered on the planet, nothing would change. He would still be J. B., as real as I am, without the curse of his own flesh obscuring his true existence. This is a cosmic riddle! It is a materialistic joke! By the time Muddyscuttlers discover genuine existence, it is too late to deal with materiality they thought was true reality.

How slow is flesh! Hordes of humans followed Moses through Muddyscuttle wastelands. Time and again the High Command performed magnificent miracles for them. He split seas, gave water from stone, and fed them bread from the desert floor! Did they believe, having seen? Not for long. They died in the wilderness in aching blindness.

The miracle of the humanization alone should produce faith. He divided loaves, walked the waters, and drew the dead from coffins and tombs. His reward for all this was not belief, but humiliation and execution. At His death we in Upperton did not cry over the mutilation of His flesh—we knew that for what it was. It was the insult to love that left our High Command reaching in agony from the Crystal Chair.

Some Scuttlers used to debate the question: Do miracles create faith, or does faith create miracles? Their question is absurd. Miracles transcend science and reason in demonstrating the supernatural realm. Most are reclaimed before they gain any perception of this realm. They meet the Logos before they ever learn the significance of miracles. I must not despair. J. B. will be better motivated toward reclamation by his own sense of need than by Aunt Ida's miracle.

When I am discouraged, I think of this. During the humanization, our Lord said, "If I be lifted up, I will draw all men to Myself." It is not by little miracles, great arguments, nor threatening circumstances that men come to life everlasting. Life is the Logos, eternal in power, pervading the cosmos, indwelling materiality. The great miracle is this reduction. Life is the great Agent encamping in small spirits.

"The Logos is the Lodestone." He will draw. I feel that J. B. may already be caught in His web of life. Let us wait and see if he may not soon experience the only great miracle there is—the transformation of pitiful mortality into eternal life.

In the meantime I must clear the debris from the rails. Assail the barriers. Desire. Wait.

> *One miracle alone exists—*
> *When He has come to be*
> *The Author of a higher life*
> *And immortality.*

Alleluia,
Valiant

The Month
of the Logos

I am coming to understand that faith is a matter of hearing. Words have immense power over mortals since they form the fabric of all reason. Cleveland is under seige by a new and powerful word that Frankie Williams calls the Word of God. This word is now the subject of the press, and all souls who dwell in these environs seem stirred to stop and listen to it.

The Frankie Williams Conquest is in full swing, and my client has gone for the past three nights. Beau Ridley has been taking him to the Conquest, and Joymore and myself have derived great pleasure from these experiences. You may think me planetbound, but these stadium services seem to smack of Upperton. Each night thirty thousand Scuttlers sing and pray for the reclamation of Cleveland. Best of all, there are thirty thousand guardians present, too. It is the best angelic singing I have heard since I left Cogdill. They are a superb evidence of what Couriers Elite can really do in the spiritual atmosphere of a fallen world. I know I have often railed upon the quality of religious music, but I have made an interesting discovery: one reason why mortal hymns are so bad is that mortals sing them. The melodies, harmonies, and words are really quite beautiful when properly sung by our own kind.

The Conquest Songster is a fine human singer as he leads his stadium congregation. His guardian, Constellation, has been leading the Couriers in the better music. If these Scuttlers could hear us, they might have an immediate experience of grace. Some of their hymns have dreadful lyrics that speak of human depravity and destitution. They really do not apply to the Couriers, but we sing them anyway. Here is a good example of their not-so-angelic lyrics:

> Just as I am and waiting not
> To cleanse my soul of one dark blot
> To Thee whose blood can cleanse each spot
> O Lamb of God, I come!

But to mortals with low ways, such lyrics are not so outlandish as they seem. Such ideas definitely need consideration.

Frankie Williams is a good evangelist. His words sear the human conscience. More than five hundred Scuttlers were reclaimed as the choir sang about human sin and spots and blots. How wholesome for them to consider their estate before our Beloved! Few such moments of truth and light occur upon this dismal orb.

Cleveland is aglow with a strange light. The High Command must have been overjoyed to see five hundred reclaimed at a single service. I doubt whether Upperton can imagine anything like this stadium full of men and angels joined in song. It was so ecstatic that we sang our way out of the arena and into the parking lots in a baptism of light.

Fervent angelic singing rose from those guardians whose clients were reclaimed. I wanted so to join them, but J. B. would not go forward. He listened to Frankie Williams, but refused to budge all through the entreaty.

At one point J. B. appeared almost repentant and seemed as moved as he was the night Aunt Ida left him alone in the hospital room. He had resolved not to go forward and so clung to the stadium seat before him. He gripped the iron rail until his knuckles whitened. If he had released it for only a moment, he might have come to faith.

He is struggling against the Logos, but he is losing. He is being propelled to faith by a motivation stronger than I alone could compel him. He is caught in the irresistible magnetism of the Lodestone.

Now, about his romance.

Today he finally called Cassie. She seemed pleasant, but declined his offer of a lift to the Conquest tonight. Because she declined, he has decided to stay home. I am disappointed in this decision. J. B. is so close, and I desperately hope that Clockstop will be stayed until he is safely reclaimed.

One important incident you must know about. Yesterday J. B. and I had lunch with Beau Ridley and Nova. Beau talked to J. B. of Logos' life. He used a tool that the Committee will deplore—the Thessalonian Turnpike. I hope you will not think ill of Beau, for he does it with his whole heart. While I don't like the concept in general, it had a powerful effect.

Beau's earnest entreaty came cloaked with clichés. While he lacked John McDonald's self-righteousness, his witness sounded similar:

"J. B., tell me this. Have you come to the place in your spiritual life that you know for sure if you were to die right now, you could be holding a harp instead of a pitchfork?"

"Well, I suspect it would be the latter," answered J. B. "All I know is that since I have been attending the Frankie Williams Conquest, I have been confused."

"That is just my point, J. B. Why do you think God had you and me become friends?"

"Was it God who did that? I didn't know that! I thought it just sort of happened because we both work for the same company and eat in the same lounge."

"No, J. B.! I've never found things that happenstance. God has a definite plan for even those events that seem small and insignificant." Beau seemed to speak with the tone of a bishop. "Everything that happens to us, God engineers in such a way to get us out from under our circumstances and put us under the blood."

"Under the blood? That's an unpleasant idea," objected J. B. "Besides, how can God, who is busy doing all the things He has to get done, manage to care about International Investors, much less the man in Cubicle 32?"

"The gospel is the great plan of a holy God. He wants everyone to get to know Jesus Christ. J. B., have you ever considered receiving Jesus as your personal Savior and getting saved by the blood?" Beau spoke in churchese, but J. B. responded in good faith.

"Oh, Beau, I don't know that much about God. At Grace Church and at the Conquest I think about the idea, but it looks impossible for me. Faith is easier for people like you than it is for those like me."

"Nonsense, J. B.!" protested Beau. "All things are possible through prayer. God can do anything but fail. You should really go after Jesus, 'cause where you go hereafter depends on what you go after here." Again the clichés flew.

"Sure. But it would be hard." J. B. was painfully honest. "I don't think I could be a good Christian even if I tried. I could never be as dedicated as you are, Beau. I've seen the changes in Cassie. I don't think I have the stuff it takes. Even if I could really make up my mind about God, I just don't think I could hold out, no matter how hard I tried."

"You don't have to hold out, and you don't have to try. Just quit trying and start trusting,"

Beau said. "Now, let me show you here from the Book of Thessalonians how you can be a part of that great Turnpike to Truth. I can show you in ten minutes how you can get out from under life's circumstances and get under the blood. You see, life is a matter of the Three R's."

"Reading . . . 'riting . . . and 'rithmetic?" asked J. B.

"Nope," grinned Beau, smiling that J. B. was so ignorant of the Thessalonian Turnpike. "Recognizing, Repenting, and Receiving. First you recognize your lost condition. Then you repent of your sin, and then you can receive the gospel and be saved by the blood."

"I'd like to believe in the Book of Thessalonicans —" said J. B. seriously, mispronouncing the word.

"Thessalonians! THESSALONIANS!" Beau corrected.

"Yes, but right now I've got more important things to consider."

"J. B., there are no more important things than to believe the Three R's and save your soul from an eternal Devil's Hell. . . ."

That is how it went. Beau's concern expressed itself in clichés. He is deeply earnest about it all, however. J. B. appears anxious to be "under the blood." He seems earnest, too.

I must close. J. B. has just accepted an invitation to tonight's Conquest after all. What a rapturous turn of events!

> Just as they are, they have come from the
>   night,
> Invading infinity, dwelling in light.
> From the kingdom of graves and realms of the
>   dead
> They have turned to the day spring of life.

Alleluia,
Valiant

On the Way to the Conquest

Well, here we are in the automobile on the way to the Conquest. I know I am still trying too hard, for I am overwrought in my preoccupation with J. B.'s anxieties. The Lord High Command created me without a nervous system so that I would not be subject to the feelings of Muddyscuttlers, but my client could be near a decision.

I am learning to love him more every day. I accept this crescendo of affection, knowing that it is the order of things. The love of the angels ever grows more ardent, constantly expanding like the love of the Great Chair itself.

Some angels hold to the theory of ultimate unity. The theory teaches that spiritual beings have a life destined to converge with life once begun in the material world. This means that in time, spirituality and all being will intersect on a new plane of reality where men and angels are indistinguishable. The quality of life which results will transcend current existence as being finally surpasses all remembrance of flesh. In one transcendent moment, the last vestiges of biology will be abandoned forever. While I have not decided about ultimate unity, I believe that one day we can expect a merger of the Glorifex Factor with this expansion of love.

I cannot tell if the resulting glory-love will continue parallel to spirit or intersect it in a new category of transcendence. There will be no cleavages in this unfolding glory. It will proceed in orderly fashion from one plateau of glory to the next. But who can predict its quality, intensity, or nature in the uncharted anguria ahead? It will never stop. Upperton shall not ever restrict this infinite unfolding. If J. B. could know and taste a morsel of such grandeur and ecstasy! If he could but suspect it, I could leave the Scuttle in the joy of my achievement.

I gasp at human possibilities. J. B. has the possibility of grandeur we never can experience: reclamation. Can you imagine? Beginning existence contaminated as flesh and ending in effulgent love. Scuttlers taste grace, while we only know what it is like to be loved in foundational purity. But they know the glory of love that comes in spite of contamination. Ah, to be lifted from dank materiality by the loving hand of the Lord High Command! I hope soon to enter into the full joy of my client.

I must turn from this glorious philosophy to one more mundane. I wonder if I have the proper attitude toward the Conquest. Does the High Command intend for us to make this an angelic sing-a-long?

My definition of ecstasy may be faulty. There is a basic difference between human and angelic joy: Human joy can exist in the interest of humans themselves; angelic joy is selfless. Scuttlers sometimes praise to feel good. Sometimes they feel good and thus praise. But they never praise as a basic part of their nature as we do.

Humans can abuse praise. Instead of reflecting the glory of the Logos, they praise sometimes just to escape the depression of Muddyscuttle. It serves as a kind of mood displacement. It is the duty of man to praise the High Command as it is the duty of guardians. Still, much of human praise serves the creature and not the Creator.

Even knowing its flaws, I have come to esteem human praise, though I cannot tell why. Is such esteem related to the Conquest? When I attended Grace Church, I was less impressed with their praise. Now I wonder whether it was because the number who gather in Grace Church is smaller than the Conquest crowd. Scuttlers themselves are prone to evaluate the success of religious meetings by the number in attendance. It is a shallow habit. I must be careful not to measure the meaning of joy by volume alone.

Daystar seeks to turn humans from the will of the Logos by reminding them regularly of the importance of group approval. I have noticed during my tour that planetlings have an uncommon concern over what others think and feel. Few Scuttlers are at home with their uniqueness. I cannot fathom this, since the High Command creates everything with great variety and desires versatility in every quadrant of the cosmos. Yet here, upon this blue ball, they are slow to recognize and esteem their individuality.

Conformity rules on Muddyscuttle. What one wears, all must wear. What one owns is an incentive to the hordes to possess the same thing. Even so-called nonconformists shudder to think that their nonconformity may be an unpopular sort. Each must somehow find approval in the mass.

Daystar told Adam and Eve they could break their commitment to the Great Chair and become like the High Command themselves. Of course, this was untrue. But the temptation was the words "become like." From that time to this, these have been the key words in social identity. But why would angels at the Conquest participate so eagerly? One hopes we are not becoming populist and believe that the greater the number, the more significant the gathering.

One principle extends from this one. Real intercourse and fellowship with the Logos occur only in isolation. Scuttlers are created to be communal, and so it will ever be. But solitude is the highest path of communication between worlds. Many times during the humanization of Logos He set the example by withdrawing from the masses to talk alone with Upperton. Few humans are comfortable in being alone. I know that loneliness can be the worst of human pain, but I have a distaste for their absurd fetish for constant togetherness and the feeling that big groups produce big relationships with God.

There is nothing so counterspiritual as constant accompaniment. J. B. must drop this assumption. His fascination with the mass assembly lies in his need for personal identity. There is truth in the human cliché: "A man is known by the company he keeps." In the context of his relationships, each man finds the definition of himself.

This is not the finest self-definition, for it is purely sociological, a distorted reflection, an image in a comic mirror. The best self-image comes when they look, not outward to the crowd, but inward to the spirit. For J. B. this discovery lies out ahead.

The Logos knew it was impossible to help people if you are always with people. His great inwardness was best manifest at His execution. As His suffering there grew so intense, it might have obscured communication. But the communion He had learned in solitude supplied Him with the necessary strength for His ordeal. Divine intimacy brought strength.

I know my concern is legitimate. They have been publishing Conquest attendance in the daily papers. Somehow J. B. feels a great deal of pride in this. It excites him to be part of such a venture.

The success syndrome in the Christian enterprise that fascinates J. B. bothers me. He watches Frankie Williams with such adulation, it is as though he has just seen a resurrected saint. In his misplaced esteem, again he is confusing "bigness" with "greatness."

It disturbs me that he has so little adulation for Grace Church. By contrast with the Conquest, the church appears small and unimpressive. This is unfortunate, for much of the human dedication at Grace Church is beautiful. It has all that the Conquest offers plus a spiritual rapport that is warm and affirming.

Possibly an illustration would be helpful. I cannot expect you to understand baseball. It amuses me only because it keeps guardians flying over a large grassy area to stay near their clients. They must feel as I do when J. B. and I are on the tennis court—a frenzied act of guardianship I must not try to describe.

I distract myself . . . where was I . . . oh, yes, now I remember. Baseball teams are divided into leagues. Those that hold less interest are referred to as the Minors. Well, J. B. is giving the Conquest Major League esteem, and Grace Church, Minor.

I regret that I am earthbound in my illustration. I hope mortal esteem for Williams does not stop humans from loving the Logos. Misplaced admiration thrives on Muddyscuttle. Still, the evangelist seems worthy of the confidence placed in him. He is a man snared in the web of his calling. He does not covet prestige. He has strength without arrogance in spite of the Major League status forced upon him by others. Whatever I might say of Williams, he plays a critical role in my client's hoped-for reclamation. I trust that when he leaves the city, Grace Church will continue the progress the Conquest made with Considine.

EVELASCO

I have become aware that the Logos draws men to Himself. The universal love of the High Command designs the best circumstances to guide men to destiny. I see what J. B. cannot see—that he is not alone in his struggle. He thinks that everything depends on himself. He thrashes like a new swimmer making a desperate crossing. The Logos endured the agony of death for the hope of my client. He has erected a thousand barriers of love to keep him from traveling his hapless way to nothingness. I thrill at the thoroughness of His love. To end in Daystar's pit, J. B. must struggle over a hundred barricades of grace. Think of the obstacles the High Command has already laid in J. B.'s path to self-destruction: Aunt Ida, McDonald, Beau Ridley, Grace Church, Cassie, Frankie Williams, and even the biopsy. But Cassie is the key.

Cassie is preparing to attend a spiritual renewal weekend when the Conquest is over. She and many other singles will travel on chartered buses to a mountain retreat for extensive Bible study and prayer. As for Cassie and J. B., their relationship cannot maintain this distance much longer. They are clearly in love. Cassie consumes his thinking. Alphalite says Cassie has intense reciprocal feelings.

The last reckoning is desperate and close for my client. J. B. must come to know the Logos, and soon. Divine affection is constantly thwarted by glandular romantic trivia. Humans rarely seek higher affection if a lower one is accessible.

Human love is, indeed, powerful if only to humans. Nonetheless, I may have given such love a lower rating than it deserves. It is unfortunate that I lived so closely with the gluttonous sexual side of romance during my first assignment on the planet. In the case of J. B. and Cassie, this sweaty, grunting facsimile may at last have risen from its muddy roots to become a demonstration of divine love.

What of J. B.'s love for Williams? Call it esteem, if you will. Still, J. B.'s reverence for the evangelist may be more natural than I should like to admit. Humans tend to admire those who assist the Logos in reclamation. I was aghast that Ridley approached my client with the Thessalonian Turnpike. Yet it accents the substance of the Logos' last command. But it could be better done on the basis of experience and appeal. Beau Ridley, like other Scuttlers, is not very far advanced in his spirituality. He uses mechanistic and mundane cybernetics with great zeal. But soon Frankie Williams will no longer be in Cleveland, and I may then be glad that Beau is working with J. B. in any way.

I realized only today that Miltie has reached the age of Advanced Knowledge. He must shortly be told the saga of Daystar. This is a difficult tale for cherubs. Knowing the truth of this sordid rebellion is as close as Upperton comes to sadness. I don't know who has been elected to tell him of pride, and freedom, and the danger of angelic egoism. I wish he did not have to know, but he must. It is the code of Upperton.

I am sure that by now Miltie has learned of my affairs on this planet. He has always shown great interest in the work of all the Couriers. I'm sure he knows now of my progress with J. B. Miltie must look forward to the kind of service I am now rendering.

I cannot believe, however, that Miltie will ever serve on the Scuttle. There is a general feeling that Clockstop is at hand. It is a common error of men to try and wrest the secret of this conclusion from the sealed vault of the High Command. We consider this cosmic presumption. Every age of man has seen and known prophets with specific dates. An old angel called these fiery prophets "doomsday dolts." I must not join these Scuttlers in their cosmic presumption. Miltie might, after all, walk the planet with a client of his own.

Of course, by that time J. B. will either be in Upperton or in Daystar's chamber. It is my desire—and all of Cogdill's—that he shall be with us. To this end Upperton waits and watches.

> *Comes now the great and holy state,*
> *The promise beckons us to wait.*

Alleluia,
Valiant

The Triumph

Hallelujah! Reluctance has been slain! J. B. has been set free from the bonds of Daystar! It happened at the Conquest on the last night that Frankie Williams was in town. It is difficult to tell of the soul-struggle J. B. encountered.

As he made his public commitment, all my fears of spurious identity were allayed. Neither the size of the crowd nor Frankie Williams was much in his mind at the time of his reclamation. Glorious truth! Wherever true reclamation occurs, it is always a highly individual matter. Although he stood before the Conquest crowd, it seemed to J. B. that he and the Logos were the only two in Cleveland.

His joy can hardly be described! He is filled with peace and a feeling of enlightenment. His whole being seems to have a quality of richness—a new wealth that derives from his spiritual inheritance. There are many aspects to this.

First, he has acquired the wonderful inwardness that is the inviolate principle of Upperton. This inwardness is not *sui generis*. He has created neither its being nor its value. It is the substance of an invasion that has flooded his life, through the narrowest opening of his will. He desired this inwardness only in little amounts, but it came in torrents. The flood has dumfounded him with light. He willed it all, and yet there is so much more than he willed.

Joy is so innate to us that I can barely understand its impact, first discovered. These who have been born empty come to fulness in a deluge of mood that is a visible evidence of the existence of our realm. I assume it is not the only evidence of the Logos that this planet can boast, but it is dynamic.

There is an element of exhibitionism in it. J. B. sings constantly these days. His vocal quality is as poor as his spirit is rich. Thankfully, his musical expression is covert. He reserves it for himself and the angels. He sings in the shower—a common human tendency I do not claim to understand. But it is new to my client since his joy came upon him. It is not sterile joy. He has an interest in Bible reading that is spontaneous, no longer motivated by the memory of Aunt Ida, and he has not been stopped once by the "begat" passages.

He is making a marked effort toward personal reform. He has questioned himself about almost every form of indulgence that he once permitted. He is viewing gluttony and drunkenness, lust and jealousy from a new perspective. The accursed "girlie books" are all gone now . . . even those he considered the best. He has canceled a planned trip for rest and relaxation which was to include the loosest sort of activities. He no longer uses the name of the High Command in Muddyscuttle phrases. But most impressive of all is a formidable mental discipline with which he garrisons his thoughts.

It is spring on Muddyscuttle now, and even I am taken with the beauty of life. The greens and blues of planets such as this have a beauty and charm all their own. There are still evidences of the fall of man all about . . . bits of

rusted steel, candy wrappers, and decaying beverage cans. Yet a strong feeling of salvation garners new life from buds about to break into flowers. This feeling blankets the fields and hills. I wonder how it all would have looked without the contamination of Daystar. How foolish Adam was to blight his world for the slithering proposition of his deceiver.

The world seems so new that I can scarcely believe I have been on the planet for years. I wish J. B. would go into the country alone to celebrate his new joy and leave me dumfounded on the warm earth. It is not the pigsty I had first thought. Now, in the explosion of spring, I understand how our Beloved felt. I know at last why the High Command so loved the orb that He permitted the humanization.

Alas, I cannot understand why my client is still struggling with his lower nature. He noticed Cassie in church yesterday during a less captivating moment of the sermon. His mind descended rapidly below his higher nature. He was almost engulfed in the lust he experienced when they were living together. It was seething, if unexpressed. Yet he maintained a reverent look as a masquerade.

As I looked around, all the other Scuttlers in pew twenty-eight looked the same way, and I was hit by a cold chill. The ghastly indulgences behind all those pious looks! Had I pores, I should have sweated.

Soon the pastor spoke a sharper thought, and J. B. left his fantasies and returned to his old sweet self, as they say down here. I was alarmed —the self was not so sweet after all. His hypocrisy was instant and stifling. He could feel his gluttony while appearing to be lost in the adoration of the Logos.

His lust was intense and real. I did not imagine it. He experienced it all right in church. It has left me with a strange foreboding, and I cannot stay my fears. Are my hopes to be dashed by his permissive mind?

Further, while friends rejoice over his reclamation, I fear that Grace Church may dilute his
zeal. He is being rushed all at once to join too
many church organizations. He has been asked
to join two choirs, two Sunday school classes,
the bowling league, the men's club, the discus-
sion team, and the Saturday Night Meet-A-
Friend Club. Should he try to join all, he will be
all legs and no heart in a short time. He has so
far resisted the recruiters, but I don't know how
long he can hold out.

I fear that this new fervor may be diverted to
secondary allegiances. I shudder to think he
might join so many good causes and yet miss
the best.

> *Die blight*—
> *Flee night*—
> *Grow sight*—
> *Come light!*

Alleluia,

Valiant

The New Duty

There is a touch of naïveté in my joy. It is far too similar to J. B.'s. I am the guardian of an imperfect being. He is still a mortal and in need of daily grace. Before I left Upperton I was instructed in two graces. Reclaiming grace is the initiation into life. It is rich, wonderful, and transforming.

But alone it is not adequate. I remember one other instruction: It is possible to have eternal freedom, yet be in slavery to the times. Daily grace issues from saving grace. Both are the constant application of the principle of obedience. As reclamation grace brought J. B. to the Logos, now daily grace continues his relationship. This continuance is witnessed in a continual communion and forgiveness. It is fueled by confession that cannot be made only once.

To live under Logos control is the whole duty of man. J. B. must constantly submit himself to this control. Indeed, he must live with confession on the tip of his tongue. Confession will serve him in two ways. First, it elevates the Logos moment by moment. Only when He is lifted to the apex of human esteem will other values fall in proper place. Perspective results.

The other attribute of confession is that the Logos becomes the sentinel of the mind. The mind is not a broad sea, but a narrow channel that admits but one thought at a time to pass its choppy waters. If the Logos controls the channel of thought, there is no room for insidious gluttonies and sins to swim in the narrows of awareness. J. B. must learn that impish thoughts play by permission. Only if he gives them channel space will they swim and dive, cavort and play.

I once imagined that J. B.'s reclamation would be the end of my struggles. He, too, labored under the same illusion. Both of us must abandon this unrealistic view. J. B.'s name is now recorded in the Logos' Journal. But his experience of lust in church yet disturbs me. I must still deal daily with the immediacy of flesh.

There is a weight to be born by the reclaimed. To live in flesh and dream of spirit—that is the enigma! To confess love from lips capable of denial is a grievous burden. It produces a tension that few deal with very well. Often the reclaimed become so fond of grimdeeds that they cease to enjoy righteousness, or they become so fond of righteousness that they never again enjoy grimdeeds.

There is only one answer to J. B.'s conflicts. It is preoccupation with the Logos. In His humanization the Logos provided the key to transcend this struggle. The Logos was bone of their bone and flesh of their flesh; their hope lies in His struggle and not in their own. He is the solution to the riddle. He is the heart of the mystery: His perfection can be the same triumphant force in their lives that it was in His own.

Constant confession allows men to live in one world and cling to the values of another. There was a cliché during my first term that spoke of the people who were "so heavenly minded they were no earthly good." I fear that idea. It is false. May J. B. be so heavenly minded that he may at last be of some earthly good.

The heavenly minded man is the only one who matters. The earthly minded man is like a bird with a broken wing. He cannot rise, for he has lived close to the earth for so long, he has forgotten the nature of sky. Ah, but even worse than the loss of sky, he has lost perspective! The sky and ground become one. His soul is hobbled by a vision content with its own crippled nature.

Life has come,
Yes, life has come
And death is speechless,
Stricken dumb.

Alleluia,

Valiant

In the Bus Terminal

A week has passed since J. B.'s reclamation, and I now find myself in a bus depot. As always I have my journal with me, including copies of this document for the Committee. I carry this file with me because of the certainty of my client's termination. But I must hurriedly conclude these papers, for the time is at hand. It is time to board the bus that J. B. must ride into foreverness.

May I tell you of my client's latest joy? He and Cassie have been exploring a tentative relationship. They are here with forty or more others waiting to board a motorbus for a trip they suppose will take them to a renewal center.

J. B. is unsuspecting. For him this is an opportunity for participating in a time of Bible study. Being with Cassie has doubled his joy. He is full of promises yet unspoken to both the Logos and to Cassie. J. B. and Cassie are sitting and talking quietly about the new meaning which is so abundant in their current relationship. Their new rapport has blotted out their past affair. It is so sad that now that they openly celebrate their relationship, it is over.

Now I can accept the great wisdom of the

Committee. A divinity student would have been all wrong for me. At last I agree with my assignment. During J. B.'s struggle to become a new man I have arrived at a new plateau of angelic understanding. We have both been changed by the strange process of refining love.

I do love him. I know the High Command loves him, and we are in complete agreement. He is mine for only a few more hours. Shortly we shall both be back before the Chair. I anticipate the moment.

The chartered motorbus has pulled in and the passengers are called for. J. B. and Cassie are standing hand in hand. They are the joy of the Logos and could teach their world the glory of a good confession. Unfortunately, they are out of time. They would be grieved if they suspected they will never see Cleveland together again. It is not horror, but a delightful surprise that awaits them.

Excuse me that I've left this report so truncated. But I must go and watch these lovers safely across the chasm of mortality. I should not say that both of them will cross it. Alphalite has told me that Cassie's termination is not scheduled. I grieve for the grief that will be hers after the accident. J. B. has run out of time. But then, no matter; he can get on without it now.

> The cosmos knows laughter that scoffs the deep night
> Where light is withheld from the hungering eye,
> And the blind cry to see an unseeable light
> And gloom chokes the hope and the lingering sigh.
> Such come to the Logos and, pleading for sight,
> Learn that day is conceived in the black womb of night.

Allelulia,
Valiant